Heartland

Out of the Darkness

Heartland

∂B

Share every moment . . .

Heartland

❧

Out of the Darkness

by Lauren Brooke

SCHOLASTIC INC.

New York Toronto London Auckland Sydney
Mexico City New Delhi Hong Kong Buenos Aires

With special thanks to Gill Harvey

Library of Congress Cataloging-in-Publication data available.

ISBN 0-439-31714-2

Heartland series created by Working Partners Ltd, London.

Copyright © 2002 by Working Partners Ltd.
Published by Scholastic Inc. All rights reserved.

12   7/0
Printed in the U.S.A.   40
First Scholastic printing, February 2002

For Natacha — a good friend of Heartland

Chapter One

Sunlight glinted in the late afternoon, catching golden flecks in the filly's chestnut coat. Her nostrils quivered as she stared into the distance, detecting a scent on the breeze. Then, with a toss of her head, she wheeled in the snow and cantered toward her mother. Ducking under the mare's body, she began to suckle hungrily.

Amy watched from the gateway, reading every movement. The filly brought her head back up and nosed her mother's side, her bright eyes alert and curious.

"Here, Daybreak!" Amy called. Daybreak's head rose, listening. She stood still for an instant, then she took a few steps forward.

"That's it. Over here," Amy encouraged. Daybreak broke into a trot and approached the gateway. Amy felt her heart leap as the filly reached for her, snorting eagerly and butting Amy's arm with her velvety muzzle. Amy laid her hand on the filly's soft neck.

"I'd never have believed it," said Ty, coming to stand at Amy's side. "She's so different."

"She is, isn't she?" Amy smiled happily.

Ty was eighteen, three years older than Amy, and the only other person at Heartland who knew as much about the horses as she did. He knew exactly how difficult Daybreak had been — until Christmas the filly hadn't trusted people at all — not because she had been badly treated, but because she was born with an independent, fighting spirit. Now she was approaching Amy of her own free will.

Ty held out his hand for Daybreak to smell. She nudged it, gently blowing through her nostrils. "That's a good girl," he murmured.

"She wouldn't have let you do that a week ago," Amy said. After nursing the filly back to health from a virus, Amy had finally bonded with her. Then she had made sure that Ty and Ben, Heartland's other stable hand, spent as much time as they could with the filly.

"She's definitely comfortable around people now," Ty agreed. "You know, I think she's almost ready to go. We should start thinking about a new home for her and Melody soon."

"But she just got over her virus, Ty," Amy protested.

"And there's so much more handling work we need to do with her."

"Look at her, Amy," Ty said gently as Daybreak stretched out her nose, reaching to nibble the sleeve of his coat. "She's fully recovered. And she's not just accepting people now, she's actually *interested* in them, too."

Amy felt torn. She knew that what Ty was saying was true, but her bond with the foal still seemed so new and fragile. She didn't want to let her go — not yet.

"It's still too soon, Ty," she said. "Daybreak might be interested in people, but that's just the start. We have to be sure of her before we let her go to someone else. We need to know she really trusts us."

Ty shrugged and turned away, and Amy suddenly felt uncomfortable. Gazing into the distance, she watched as a crow landed on the far side of the paddock. Daybreak saw it, too, and broke away from them. As she cantered after the bird, she gave a high-spirited squeal.

"See?" Amy pointed out, feeling reassured. "She's still unpredictable."

Ty frowned thoughtfully. "Come on, Amy. She's just full of energy, and you know it. And anyway, the right owner would keep her on track. We can't keep Melody and Daybreak, it's against our rules. Besides, we need the stable for other horses — horses that really need our help."

Amy nodded. It was true. That was the way they worked — the way her mother had set up Heartland twelve years ago. Once horses had been treated successfully, they were always rehomed to make room for others.

"I'm not saying we should keep them." Amy sighed. "But I do think Daybreak needs a little more time." She glanced up at Ty and their eyes met, just for an instant. Amy looked away again, feeling awkward.

"Well, we don't have to decide today," said Ty after a pause. "For now, let's leave them outside while there's still some sun."

"Good idea," Amy agreed as they turned to walk back toward the stable yard. On their left, two other horses were nosing the snow in search of grass to graze in another turnout paddock.

Ty stopped at the gate. "I think I'll bring Moochie and Jake in now," he said. "They've probably been out in the cold long enough."

"OK," said Amy. "I guess that leaves me with the tack room to straighten up."

Ty grinned. Straightening up the tack room had become everyone's least favorite job. No matter how well they organized it, there just wasn't enough space. "Have fun," he said. "I might come and help you later if you're lucky."

"Yeah, right," said Amy, laughing. She continued on up the path and headed to the barn.

As she walked into the tack room, she gazed at the racks, frowning. Most of them had two or three saddles on them, and although they were placed carefully on top of one another, it really wasn't ideal. Half of another wall was taken up with the bridles, bits, and martingales, the other half with photos and show ribbons. Then there was the table where they cleaned the tack, plus the storage trunks at the back, halters, lunging equipment. . . . It was all laid out neatly enough, but there was barely room to move.

Just as she was picking up a fallen bridle, Ben came in and dumped a grooming kit into one of the trunks.

"How's it going?" he asked.

"Not so great, at the moment," Amy answered. "We need more space. I think we'll have to totally reorganize. How did Red's schooling go today?"

Red was Ben's own horse, a six-year-old chestnut gelding that was turning out to be a really talented show jumper.

"Fine. He's jumping really well." Ben was looking around as he spoke. After a moment he gestured to the left wall of the tack room. "Why don't you take down those pictures and ribbons and put up more saddle racks?"

"We could, I guess," Amy said slowly. She looked at the pictures. There was one of her on Sundance, another of her mother, Marion, on Pegasus, and a whole row of other horses that had come and gone under her mother's care. Amy didn't even remember some of them — she'd been too young. And now that both her mom and Pegasus were gone, perhaps it would be best to take the pictures down, as Ben suggested.

"Or maybe just some of them," Ben added, looking at Amy's thoughtful face.

Amy smiled quickly. "No, it's a good idea," she agreed. "I'll see how Lou and Grandpa feel about it. And find out whether we can afford more racks."

Amy headed into the farmhouse. She kicked off her boots on her way to the back room where her older sister, Lou, had set up her office. Just as Amy expected, she found Lou staring intently at the laptop in front of her.

"Hi," Amy said, peering in through the doorway. "I've just been thinking about the tack room. Ben suggested we take down the pictures and put up some new racks. It would help — for now, at least."

"What?" Lou answered absentmindedly. She started to type rapidly, her blue eyes never leaving the screen.

"New saddle racks," Amy repeated. "The tack room's so full we're having to pile saddles on top of one another."

"Oh, right," Lou said after a pause. She stopped typing for a moment, then began again. "Sounds like a good plan. We could probably find room for all of those pictures in the house anyway. How much would the racks cost?"

"I'm not sure," Amy said. "Could you find out?" She stepped into the room and peered briefly over Lou's shoulder at the laptop. "Glad you're enjoying your new toy," she teased.

"Toy!" Lou exclaimed. Unlike Amy, she'd grown up in England, and her British accent always sounded stronger when she was indignant about something. She looked up, ready to argue, but then she saw Amy's amused expression and smiled. "This is going to make a big difference, Amy Fleming. All the tedious accounting jobs will take a tenth of the time with these new programs. And we can do lots of other things, too."

She pushed the screen around so that Amy could see. "This is a database of different bedding suppliers. I'm working on a new publicity proposal. I wanted to get the wording right before showing you, but you might as well see it now."

"Publicity proposal?" Amy repeated suspiciously. "What kind of publicity?"

"For the suppliers. I've been reading about some really good bedding materials that would save you a lot of time cleaning stalls. If we allowed the suppliers to use us in their advertising material, we'd get a cheaper price," Lou explained. "And we'd benefit from the publicity, too."

"But straw's fine," Amy pointed out. "It's what we've always used."

"Yes. But the advertising would be very helpful," said Lou.

"Well, I guess so." Amy hesitated, trying to share Lou's enthusiasm. As far as she was concerned, making sure the horses were cared for was more important than any new computer equipment or advertising deal. Still, she needed to give her sister a chance. Lou had given up so much to help run Heartland. "Maybe it's worth a try," she added.

The phone rang, and Lou reached over to answer it. "Of course it is," she smiled. "You'll see."

Amy smiled back, wanting to believe her. She and Lou hadn't always seen eye to eye over the past five months since Lou had left her job in New York. But things had gradually started to get better. Now Lou belonged at Heartland as much as anyone else. Just as she headed for the door again, Amy caught a snatch of Lou's conversation on the phone.

"Well, I appreciate you getting back to me so quickly," Lou was saying. "And Sunday's absolutely fine. No problem."

There was a pause, then Lou added, "Yes, two-thirty

is fine for us, too. Yes, thank you. Good-bye." She put the phone down and turned to Amy with a smile, her cheeks slightly flushed.

"What's going on?" Amy demanded.

"Sit down," said Lou. "This is important."

"Well, OK," Amy said hesitantly. She pulled a chair up next to Lou's desk. "What is it?"

"A new client. I've found a horse that needs treating."

"A new horse?" Amy looked puzzled. "What do you mean, *you've* found one?"

"Just what I said." Lou grinned. "I've thought for a long time that maybe we should approach people directly rather than waiting for them to find us. And now I've managed to do it."

Amy was intrigued. "No kidding!" she said. "So who was it on the phone?"

"Do you remember that big fire back in November? The one at that Thoroughbred farm near Baltimore?"

Amy nodded. "Brookland Ridge," she answered. The story had been in all the papers.

"That's the one," agreed Lou. "I called them yesterday and explained who we are, and I asked whether they had any horses in need of treatment."

"But aren't they all racehorses?" Amy gasped.

"So?" said Lou. "That shouldn't be a problem, should it?"

"Well . . ." Amy paused. "I don't know. It's just that racehorses can be really high-strung and hard to deal with."

Lou's face fell slightly.

Amy took a deep breath. "You should have discussed this with me first, Lou," she said, trying not to sound annoyed.

"I'm sorry. You're right. To be honest I didn't think they'd get back to us so quickly." Lou's eyes met her sister's.

"Well, tell me about the horse." Amy sighed, trying to make the best of the situation.

Lou paused. "He's called Gallant Prince."

"Gallant Prince!" Amy exclaimed. The horse had been one of the top three-year-olds last season. He'd won the Maryland Breeders' Cup at Pimlico. Then he'd been caught in a fire and become a hero by breaking free and alerting his stable hand, who then saved many other horses. But Gallant Prince had paid a tragic price in the form of his own injuries. His tendons had been so badly damaged that he would never race again. Furthermore, he had suffered terrible burns.

"So what's happened since the fire?" Amy asked. "Did they tell you?"

Lou nodded slowly. "He went to an equine specialist center to be treated for the burns, but there's nothing more they can do for him. He's badly scarred, and he'll always be unsound. It's the emotional side that's the real problem, though. No one can get anywhere near him. I spoke to the trainer, Luke Norton, who sounded like he was at the end of his rope," Lou explained. "The fire completely traumatized the horse, and nothing they do seems to work. If we can help him, he might be able to go to stud. The owner has a farm where Prince could stay — he's so attached to the horse that he doesn't want to lose him."

"So he's a stallion." Amy thought for a moment. Gallant Prince would be an amazing horse to work with. And if she could cure him — she took a deep breath. "We'd have to keep him separate from the mares," she said.

"Can we manage that?" asked Lou anxiously.

"Let me talk it over with Ty," Amy replied.

Lou looked relieved. "Well, let me know what you decide soon," she said. "If there's a problem, I'll need to know pretty fast. I said they could bring him here on Sunday."

Chapter Two

"Ty!" Amy called, hurrying out to the yard. "Ty?"

There was no sign of him, so she headed around to the back barn.

"There you are!" said Amy, looking into Jake's stall, where Ty was unbuckling the bay horse's New Zealand blanket. Moochie was already pulling contentedly at his hay net in the stall next to him.

"What is it?" Ty asked, looking surprised at the urgency in her voice.

"Do you remember Gallant Prince? The horse up at Brookland Ridge that was caught in that terrible fire?" Amy said breathlessly.

"Of course I do," said Ty, sliding the blanket off Jake's back. "Why?"

"Well, there's a chance he could come to Heartland."

"Here?" Ty looked puzzled.

"Yeah. Lou's spoken to his trainer, Luke Norton. He's unsound, but his injuries are nearly healed. His owner wants to be able to send him to stud, but he's still completely traumatized. No one can get near him."

Ty raised an eyebrow. "I'm not surprised," he commented. "That was a pretty major thing for him to go through." He hesitated. "But do you think this is a good idea? We're not really set up to deal with racehorses here."

Amy understood his reaction. A high-strung Thoroughbred was very different from the horses they usually took on, and they were already really busy. "But we've never turned away a damaged horse before," she pointed out.

"Well, that's true," Ty agreed. He let himself out of Jake's stall with the blanket slung over his arm. "And I guess there's no real reason why we should turn away this one. It might be difficult, but . . ." He trailed off.

Amy felt relieved. "So you agree we should take him?"

"I guess it's worth a try," Ty said slowly. "We'll need to decide where to put him, though."

Amy looked down the wide aisle of the barn. There were six stalls on either side and another six in the other stable.

"He could go at the end," Amy suggested. "We could put the geldings around him." She thought quickly. Sundance, Moochie, Pirate, Jake, Crispin, Blackjack . . . and Ben's horse, Red, were all geldings. "That would leave us with one free stall. We could have that next to him, to create a gap between him and the other horses. He'd basically be on his own except for whoever was across from him. What do you think?"

"It might work," said Ty with a shrug. "It's probably the best we can do, since all the other stalls are full."

"OK," said Amy. "But I'd better check with Ben to make sure he doesn't mind moving Red."

"I'll do that," Ty offered. "And I'll bring Melody and Daybreak in, too. It's getting cold."

They walked out of the barn together. The sun had just dropped behind the white, weatherboarded farmhouse, and the light was fading. Ty headed down the path to the turnout paddocks while Amy walked back toward the house, where she could see her grandpa, Jack Bartlett, through the kitchen window. He was talking to Lou.

"Grandpa! Has Lou told you about Gallant Prince?" she asked as she came in through the door.

"She has," Jack said, smiling. "Kind of a new direction for us, isn't it?" He looked shrewdly at Amy, his eyes narrowing thoughtfully. "It's a lot to take on. You'll need to make sure he doesn't take too much of your time. Especially since Heartland will probably get a fair amount of attention over this."

"Attention?" Amy echoed.

"From the press. After all, Gallant Prince has been in the papers a lot," said Grandpa.

Amy realized that he was right. The fire at the Brookland Ridge farm and Gallant Prince's heroic role had been big news. People would be curious about what was happening to him next.

"But that won't make any difference in how we treat him," Amy said.

"No," Grandpa agreed. "Well, it shouldn't. He's a horse that needs help, like any other. But it might be difficult to remember that. You'll be under a lot of pressure, Amy."

Amy felt a pang of anxiety at his words. It was impossible to know exactly how difficult Prince was going to be without meeting him first. But they'd coped with badly traumatized horses before. She was sure it would be all right. Gallant Prince needed them. It *had* to be all right.

"Are you OK with this?" Lou asked Amy, concerned. "If you think it's too much, I can always give Mr. Norton a call."

"No," Amy said determinedly. "I'm sure we can cope. It sounds like we're Prince's last hope. We'll take him."

❧

"Where were you this morning?" Amy demanded in a low voice as Soraya slid into the desk beside her. It was Monday morning, and Soraya hadn't been on the school bus. "Do I have news to tell you!"

"Dentist," Soraya lisped back, giving a weird, lopsided smile. Looking at her, Amy realized she couldn't speak properly because one side of her face was numb. Soraya opened her schoolbag and pulled out her history books. "So what's the news?"

With one eye on the teacher, Amy grinned excitedly. "We've got a racehorse coming to Heartland," she whispered.

"A racehorse!" Soraya stared at her friend, her brown eyes wide with amazement.

Amy nodded, but just then the history teacher caught her eye. She turned back to her books. "I'll tell you later."

Soraya gave her an impatient look but turned to concentrate on what the teacher was writing on the board.

It wasn't until the bell rang that Soraya had a chance to hear the whole story. They shoved their books in their bags and headed for the door.

"So tell me," said Soraya as soon as they were in the hall.

"It's Gallant Prince," Amy answered.

"As in *the* Gallant Prince?" Soraya asked. "The one that was in the fire?"

"That's the one," said Amy. "Apparently he's become totally unmanageable since the fire. So we're taking him on."

Soraya looked impressed. "Amy, that's amazing," she began.

"What's amazing?" said a voice behind them. They looked around to see their friend, Matt Trewin — with Ashley Grant at his side. Things had been a little uncomfortable with Matt since Ashley's Christmas party, when he'd asked Amy to go out with him. Amy had felt awkward. She really liked Matt, but she thought of him as one of her best friends — not as a boyfriend. Now he was dating Ashley, whom Amy couldn't stand.

"Hey, Matt," said Soraya.

"Well, come on, what's so amazing?" demanded Matt.

Amy longed to tell him all about Gallant Prince, but she didn't want to talk to him about Heartland with Ashley standing there. Ashley's mother ran a successful stable called Green Briar, which used very different methods from Heartland's, and Ashley never missed a chance to put Heartland — or Amy — down.

"Oh, nothing much," Amy said lightly. "So who's done their biology homework?" she went on, changing the subject.

"Why? Want some help from Matt? Now there's a surprise," Ashley said sarcastically.

Amy stared at her. Matt and Soraya never minded helping her out when she was short of time, and it was none of Ashley's business. "I've finished it, actually," Amy retorted.

"That *is* news!" Matt grinned teasingly.

He and Ashley sauntered off, and Amy shook her head as she watched them go. She still didn't understand why Matt liked Ashley so much. She was awful! But he just didn't seem to see it.

"*Have* you finished your homework?" Soraya asked when they were out of earshot.

"Of course not," said Amy. "Can you give me a hand?"

"Sure thing." Soraya smiled. "We'll do it at lunch."

But even with Soraya helping her, Amy had trouble concentrating that day. Her mind kept drifting back to the stallion. What would he be like? How badly damaged would he be? She tried to imagine the terror of a horse caught in a fire, and shuddered. It would take a long time for any horse to recover from that. Amy pictured the beautiful horse she'd seen on TV, muscles rippling as he crossed the finish line at Pimlico. Gallant Prince must look pretty different now — and feel terribly different, too. Amy wondered if he would respond to her. She wasn't sure where she was going to begin.

🙚

As Amy hurried up Heartland's long driveway that afternoon, she felt a sense of relief that the school day was over. A car passed her on the way, heading in the opposite direction. Amy turned to watch it go, then went into the farmhouse.

"Lou!" she called as soon as she entered the kitchen. "Lou? Who was that?"

"I'm in here," came Lou's voice from the living room.

Amy went in and was surprised to see the armchairs turned to face each other. Lou was putting photo albums back on the bookshelf.

"What's going on?" Amy asked.

"A reporter was here," Lou answered, looking excited. "We're going to be in the *Richmond Post.*"

"The *Richmond Post*?" Amy looked astonished.

"Uh-huh," said Lou. "And all because of Gallant Prince."

"But how did they find out so fast?" Amy gasped. "He's not even here yet."

Lou shrugged, picking up the empty coffee cups from the table. "I guess word must have leaked out at Brookland Ridge."

"So what did the reporter want to know?"

"All sorts of stuff about Heartland. How we work. About Mom, and what happened . . ."

"Well, I guess that's OK," said Amy, taking a deep breath.

"It can't do us any harm," Lou agreed, grinning.

❧

Amy tried to keep Prince in the back of her mind when she started the barn chores the next morning. She headed for Melody and Daybreak's stall first.

"Hi, girl," she said softly to Melody as she slipped a halter over Daybreak's ears. "I'm going to take your baby for a walk."

As Amy led the little filly out of the stall, Melody whinnied anxiously. Daybreak was already looking around eagerly, excited to be out. Amy led her up the yard, then asked her to stop. The foal halted obediently, and Amy began her routine of running her hands over Daybreak's body and asking her to pick her feet up, one at a time. When Daybreak was older, she'd have her hooves picked out regularly and her feet shod, so it was important that she know what to expect and get used to balancing on three legs. Daybreak was eager to please and nuzzled Amy affectionately.

"Good girl," said Amy, picking up one of her forelegs.

"She looks relaxed!" Ben commented as he came out of the feed room.

"She sure does," Amy agreed. "We're really making progress. Are you busy?"

"Well, I was going to lunge Red, but it can wait a while," he said. "Why?"

"I was wondering if you would handle Daybreak a little," said Amy. "She still needs to work more with other people."

"Sure," Ben nodded.

"Great," said Amy. "Ten or fifteen minutes will be plenty. It might be better if I'm not around, but if you need me, I'll be in the tack room."

"OK," Ben said, taking the lead rope. "I'll come find you if I need you."

Amy headed into the crowded tack room. She realized that she hadn't had time to ask Grandpa how he felt about moving the pictures and made a mental note to have a talk with him later. She was just working up a shine on Sundance's saddle when Ty peered in. Amy met his gaze and smiled. They'd hardly seen each other all week — there had been so much to do.

"How's it going?" he asked softly.

"Not bad," said Amy. "I worked Daybreak a little, and now Ben's with her. You're moving the geldings today, aren't you?"

She reached out for the saddle soap, but it slipped and fell to the floor near Ty's feet. He picked it up and stepped closer to hand it back. Amy took it from him,

blushing slightly. She had a feeling that Ty had been trying to find a quiet moment to talk to her ever since
Christmas Eve, when they'd kissed. But she didn't know
what to say. Ty was really special to her, and his kiss had
made her heart pound, but she wasn't sure what it all
meant. And the last thing she wanted was to be like the
other girls at school, obsessing over a boyfriend all the
time.

"Amy —" Ty began.

"Ty, I —" she started at the same time. They both
stopped and looked at each other.

"Amy, I think Daybreak's had enough," Ben's voice
came from the doorway, making them both jump. "Shall
I put her in her stall?"

"No, I can do that," Amy said, feeling relieved at the
interruption. "Was she OK with you?" She brushed
gently past Ty and stepped back into the yard.

"Yeah, she was fine," said Ben. "Melody's looking
kind of stressed, though."

Amy turned to see Melody peering over her half door,
craning her neck anxiously to keep an eye on her daugh-
ter. "She'll be OK now," said Amy. She knew she should
go back into the tack room and have that talk with Ty,
but something stopped her — something was holding
her back. If they talked, something might change. Somehow it seemed a whole lot easier to keep things just the
way they were — the way they'd always been. Taking

hold of Daybreak's halter, she led the filly back to her stall.

By the time Amy had taken off Daybreak's halter and come out of the stall, Ty was already leading Pirate out of the yard toward the back barn. Amy bit her lip. She regretted not talking to him, and a little voice inside her whispered, *Something has already changed*. Pushing the thought to the back of her mind, she quickly returned to the tack room. There really was too much to do. She'd have to think about Ty later. . . .

By late morning, Amy was starving. Heading into the kitchen in search of food, she realized that Lou was on the phone. It sounded like she was talking to Scott Trewin, her boyfriend. He was Matt's brother, and the local equine vet. Opening the fridge, and hunting for something that would make a good lunch, Amy tried not to listen to the conversation.

"It's *not* that, Scott," Lou was saying in a heated voice. "It's nothing personal. You have to see that."

It wasn't like Lou and Scott to argue, and Amy felt embarrassed overhearing her sister. "At least it *is* a system," she heard Lou say next. "And if it's going to work, we have to apply it to everyone. Why does it bug you so much?"

As she put some ham and a slab of the cheese on the

table, Amy spotted the *Richmond Post* on the counter. She reached for the paper eagerly and started leafing through it to find the article on Heartland. Lou hung up the phone and sat down. "It's on page four," she told Amy, still sounding annoyed from the phone call. She paused. "I just don't know why Scott's making such a fuss."

Amy looked up. "Making a fuss? About what?"

"Oh, I sent out letters to all our creditors, saying that from now on Heartland would pay all bills at the end of the month," Lou said. "You know — just a standard form letter. Scott says he'd rather stick with the old system, so I said there wasn't really what I'd call a system before. And now there is, and he's part of it."

"Well," Amy began cautiously, "Scott has been Heartland's vet for years."

"Yes, I know," said Lou, sounding exasperated. "But this is much more efficient."

Amy looked doubtfully at her sister. She wasn't sure what to say. She turned to the paper again and spotted the article. *Final Bets on Gallant Prince,* ran the headline. The article continued:

Since the fire that destroyed half of Brookland Ridge, the hero of the night, Gallant Prince, has been impossible to handle. His only hope lies in a training stable called Heartland. Here, it's claimed, even the wildest horses are pacified.

Amy frowned. Heartland was much more than a training stable — and she didn't really like the word "pacified," either. Gaining a horse's trust was about building a relationship, not just forcing a horse to calm down. She read on.

Heartland was established twelve years ago as a center for damaged horses by Marion Fleming, who died tragically last year. Despite her death, work at Heartland has continued. With this prestigious new arrival, all eyes will be on the stable. Heartland's reputation may rise or fall, depending on how it manages the traumatized stallion, one of Baltimore's local heroes.

Amy looked up, appalled. "This is terrible!" she exclaimed. "Our reputation may rise or fall?"

"I know." Lou sighed. "They just picked out what they wanted to hear."

A knot of anxiety clutched at Amy's stomach. "Grandpa's right. They sure know how to put the pressure on, don't they?"

Chapter Three

"If any journalists turn up before Gallant Prince arrives, don't let them in," Grandpa warned. "He's going to be worked up enough from the trip as it is."

"Don't worry," Lou reassured him. "If any more show up, we'll send them away. It'll be easier once he's here. We can shut the gates."

"Interest will probably die down once he's settled in," Amy added. "They won't want to be hanging around the stables just waiting for something to happen."

"No," Grandpa agreed. He looked around the table, where everyone had gathered for Sunday lunch. "We all need to be clear, though, that we're keeping publicity to a minimum from now on. One newspaper article's enough."

"Sure," said Ty. "That makes sense." Beside him, Ben nodded.

Amy let out a sigh of relief. She was glad that Grandpa was being so firm about this. But she was still nervous and didn't really feel much like eating. She pushed her roast chicken to one side and put her knife and fork down.

"OK, well, I'm heading back out," said Ty, clearing his throat. "I'll make sure I'm around at two-thirty."

He walked over to the door and put his boots on, and Lou started clearing the table. Ben and Amy got up to help her.

"Leave this to me," said Lou. "You head out. You've got enough to do in the yard."

✍

The trailer arrived promptly. As Amy heard it rumbling up the driveway, Lou appeared from the farmhouse. It stopped just inside the stable yard. Two men got out, one in his fifties, the other about Ty's age. Amy guesed the younger one was a stable hand.

"Louise Fleming?" asked the older man.

Lou stepped forward. "That's me," she said.

"Luke Norton," said the man, shaking her hand. "We spoke on the phone."

Lou nodded and smiled, then immediately turned to

indicate Amy and Ty. "This is my sister, Amy Fleming, and this is Ty Baldwin. They'll be looking after Gallant Prince."

Luke Norton turned to them, looking them over. "So who'll be treating him?" he asked.

"That's what I meant — Ty and Amy will," Lou said quickly.

Luke Norton raised an eyebrow and ran a hand impatiently through his thinning hair, then shrugged. "Well, as long as you're up to it. Where's Prince going to be stabled?" he went on.

"In the back barn," said Ty.

"OK." Luke Norton nodded, then turned to the stable hand. "Let's get him out, Sam." The boy nodded and started to undo the bolts on the horse trailer.

Amy watched Sam anxiously, half-listening to Luke Norton, who had folded his arms and launched into a description of the accident.

In her mind's eye, Amy saw the fire. She heard the horses whinnying, saw their eyes rolling, the smoke making them frantic with panic . . . and Prince rearing up through the flames to break down his door, his hooves splintering the wood, his terror growing as the heat intensified. . . .

The noise of the ramp being lowered brought Amy back to attention. She stepped forward and looked into the dark interior, feeling puzzled. She had expected to hear the stamping of hooves at least, but it was completely quiet inside the trailer. Sam appeared at the top of the ramp, leading the stallion. Amy was astonished. Prince didn't seem remotely unmanageable. If anything, he seemed placid and gentle as he descended gingerly, limping with each step.

Amy swallowed. The beautiful racehorse she remembered from Pimlico was barely recognizable. There was a long scar down the right side of his face, and the burned areas on his forelegs and shoulder were clearly visible. She turned quickly to Luke Norton.

"He seems very quiet. Is he tranquilized?"

Luke nodded. "It's the only way we could get him to travel."

Amy exchanged a quick glance with Ty. Of course — it made sense. If Prince was as traumatized as they said, it would be dangerous to take him anywhere in a trailer without something to keep him calm. As Sam brought the horse to a halt in front of them, she studied his lowered head and dull, spiritless eyes, then she stepped forward to gently touch his face with its zigzag white scar.

"Prince," she whispered. He stared at her dully and took several steps back.

"There's a boy," said Sam, "steady."

Prince stood still again, his head drooping.

Amy looked at Sam. "Are you his stable hand?" she asked.

Sam shook his head and looked awkward. "No, that was Ryan Bailey's job. He used to look after Prince."

"Used to?" Amy echoed.

"Ryan's left the farm," Luke Norton broke in, and then, as if that was all there was to say, he turned to Sam. "OK, let's get him stabled before he starts acting up."

Ty and Amy showed Sam the way to the back barn and let Prince into his stall. The stallion shifted his weight off his damaged leg and nosed unenthusiastically at his hay net. The geldings, in their stalls farther up the barn, sensed the presence of the new arrival and whinnied excitedly, but Prince barely flicked an ear in their direction.

"Good boy," Amy said softly. She turned to Sam again. "There's no sign of the tranquilizer wearing off yet," she said. "Do you know what he was given?"

"Yeah. It was an ACP. We gave it to him a couple of hours ago, just before we left."

"It should wear off in another couple of hours then," Ty observed.

"Probably," said Sam. "And when it does, watch out."

"What do you mean?" Amy asked quickly.

"He gets pretty wound up," Sam said, sounding serious. "I don't know what anyone can do for him, to be honest." He shrugged. "I'll get the rest of his stuff. Where do you want me to put it?"

"I'll show you," said Ty. "The tack room is in the other barn."

Amy and Ty followed Sam back to the trailer. Amy joined Lou, who was still talking to Luke Norton. "We just can't predict how long we'll need to keep him here," she was saying politely. "Each horse's needs are different. We have to get to know them individually and find out what's best for them. But we'll definitely let you know how we're doing."

"OK. Whatever's necessary," said Luke. "I'll let Mr. Hartley know. He's the owner." He shrugged. "He's the one paying for all this."

"We'll be in touch," Amy assured him.

"Yeah, well, good luck with him," Luke said briefly. "He can be a bit difficult."

He turned toward the trailer to check on Sam, who had finished unloading and was lifting the ramp back into place.

"Ready when you are, Sam," said Luke. He jumped up into the driver's seat and started the engine. Sam clambered up beside him with a wave, and Luke turned the trailer around.

"I wonder exactly what they mean by difficult?" Amy mused as the trailer disappeared down the winding drive.

Ty shrugged. "I guess we'll have to wait and see," he said as they headed back to the barn.

They turned the corner to the barn and looked into Gallant Prince's stall. Amy studied the racehorse's slender face. His fine lines suggested a deeply sensitive, receptive personality. It was hard to believe that he was really that unmanageable.

"We can work on treating his physical wounds to start with. Pain always makes any other problems worse," said Ty.

"Scott's coming this afternoon to check him over," Amy told him. "We can ask him what he thinks."

Scott arrived an hour later and whistled in disbelief as he studied the stallion's scars. He entered Prince's stall and gently ran his hand down his damaged forelegs. The stallion shifted but otherwise didn't react.

"He's still tranquilized," Scott commented. "Can we walk him out?"

"Sure," said Amy. "I'll lead him."

In the yard, Scott studied the stallion's uneven, cautious movements.

"Well, the actual injuries are pretty much healed," he said. "He'll always be unsound, but that shouldn't keep him from exercising. Racehorses are bred to be exercised intensively from an early age — they can get upset and restless if they're kept in. Without work they put on weight quickly, too, but it doesn't look as though Prince has done much of that." He lifted one of Prince's eyelids. The horse showed no resistance. Scott looked up. "How long has he been here?" he asked Amy.

"About an hour," said Amy.

"The tranquilizer should start wearing off in another hour or so," he said, examining the stallion's dull eyes again. "Any idea what he's normally like?"

"We haven't been told anything specific. Just that he's unmanageable," Amy admitted.

Scott looked serious. "It's difficult to tell how much of an effect the drug's had on him, but call me if you need any help when it wears off. I'd better head off now if I'm going to get through my other visits." He hesitated and then gave a wry smile. "Oh, and by the way, tell Ms. Fleming I'll send the invoice through as requested. And tell Lou I'll give her a call later — when I'm through with my evening office hours."

As the afternoon wore on, Amy and Ty checked regularly on Prince in between their other chores. Amy noticed that the new resident was getting more restless. Dark storm clouds were gathering in the sky, so dusk came early, by which time Prince was pacing anxiously around his stall.

"We're going to have to keep a close eye on him," she said to Ty. "A storm's upsetting at the best of times. We might even want to give him his feed now. And I'll add some Rescue Remedy to his water. It might calm him down."

"There might be another Bach Remedy that could help," suggested Ty. "I think Walnut Remedy should help him settle. Check what the book says, though. I haven't used it in a while."

Amy went to the feed room and mixed the stallion's feed in a bucket. Then she took a well-used book off the shelf and paged through to the index. It was her mother's guide to Bach Flower Remedies, and she and Ty referred to it constantly. *Walnut Remedy aids in adjustment to change, both circumstantial and environmental.*

Perfect, thought Amy. She looked along the shelf of little brown bottles and picked out two, putting them in her pocket. She would add four drops of Walnut Remedy and six of Rescue Remedy to Prince's drinking water. As she stepped out of the feed room, heavy drops of rain began to hit the yard. She ran to the barn, where she could already hear Prince stumbling around his stall. Just as she was about to draw back the bolt, there was a crack of thunder and the lights went out. The stalls were plunged into darkness.

Amy gasped. Suddenly, she heard a frantic whinny. Gallant Prince! In the last, fading bars of daylight, she saw the rolling whites of the stallion's eyes and the flash of his hooves as he reared up. He crashed down with his forelegs against the door of the stall and reared again, letting out another high-pitched whinny. As his forelegs smashed into the door again, Amy heard the sound of splintering wood.

Chapter Four

"Ty! *Ty!*" Amy dropped the feed bucket and raced out of the barn. "Come quick! There's been a blackout!"

Just at that moment, the power came back on. Light flooded out of the barn. Amy spun around and rushed back into the barn, where the desperate sounds of the stallion still echoed. As she approached Gallant Prince's stall, Amy could see that the horse's coat was completely covered in sweat. His face was tight with panic, his nostrils flaring red. He plunged around his stall, then reared again.

Amy caught sight of a stream of blood running down his foreleg. "Prince! Easy, boy!" she called, but the stallion took no notice.

"He's completely lost it," Amy cried breathlessly as Ty

appeared at her side. "And now it's upsetting the other horses."

Amy turned and saw Ben rushing through the barn door. "Ben!" she shouted.

"What's going on?" he called, running toward them.

"Can you take care of the other horses? Try to calm them down — we'll deal with Prince."

"Sure," said Ben, quickly grasping the situation.

Amy turned again to look at the stallion.

"We need to stand as close as possible," said Ty. "He has to know that we're not going to leave him, however long he carries on like this. He has to be able to trust us."

Amy nodded. There wasn't much else they could do. As Prince continued his blind fury in the stall, they called to him continuously, keeping their voices calm and soothing.

After another fifteen minutes he began to show signs of tiring, and his movements slowed. Eventually, he stood still, trembling, at the back of his stall, the whites of his eyes still rolling, his sides heaving.

"I'll try going in," said Amy.

Cautiously, she pulled back the bolt, and immediately the stallion plunged forward. Amy hastily rebolted the door. She and Ty stood, waiting until Prince slowed and stopped once more. Amy watched him intently for any signs of change, but the only difference was his exhaustion.

"We'd better get hold of Scott fast," said Ty. "He'll need to take a look at that leg."

"You call him," said Amy. "I'll stay here."

"OK," said Ty. "I left my cell phone in the kitchen. I'll be as quick as I can."

As Ty disappeared, Amy leaned over the half door, studying the stallion. Even though he had come to a halt, he still looked completely stressed out. What if he was always like this when he wasn't tranquilized? Amy felt her stomach knot with anxiety as she faced the prospect of being unable to do anything.

Ty reentered the barn. "Scott's stuck at Garston Farm delivering a calf. He says it'll be at least two hours."

"We'll just have to stay here with him," said Amy.

"Absolutely," Ty agreed. "Lou says she'll bring some supper out to the barn."

Amy let her breath out slowly. She realized she was trembling, the horse's distress had been so overwhelming. "Thanks," she said shakily. "If you hadn't been here —"

"Hey —" Ty stepped forward and touched her arm. "I'm always here, Amy. You know that."

Amy nodded gratefully and turned away. She didn't want to think about his words too much. Not right now. Gallant Prince had to come first. She looked back at the stallion. Despite his exhaustion, he had started to pace restlessly around his stall once more. . . .

❧

"I'm going to have to give him a shot of domo and torb," said Scott. "It's a sedative that should calm him down right away. It'll be impossible to get near his leg otherwise."

"OK," said Amy. She didn't like the idea of tranquilizing Prince again, but she could see that Scott was right — there wasn't any alternative. "Ty and I should be able to hold on to him."

"Can I help?" Lou offered.

"I think we can manage," said Amy. She and Ty held Prince's halter tightly while Scott quickly inserted the needle. Within seconds, Prince's breathing slowed and his head dropped. Scott quickly cleaned and disinfected the reopened wound on his leg and then bandaged it.

"I'll stay with him," Amy said when Scott had finished. "I'll get some blankets and sleep in the empty stall next door."

"I don't think you need to do that," Ty said gently.

"No, you look exhausted, Amy," Lou agreed.

"I can't leave him," Amy insisted. "Not after he's been so upset. And I think someone should be nearby when the drug wears off, anyway, in case he goes crazy again."

"Well, if you're sure." Ty looked doubtful.

"Of course, I'm sure. It's not the first time I've slept

out here. You should go home. We need someone to be awake and alert in the morning."

"Well, OK," Ty agreed reluctantly.

"Make sure you have your cell phone, Amy," said Lou, looking worried. "Then at least you can call any of us if you need to."

"Yes. You can call me anytime, too," said Scott. "I'd better head home now, though."

⸺

Amy slept badly. Prince didn't freak out again, but he woke her up in the middle of the night by pacing restlessly around his stall. As soon as it began to get light, she got up to check on him. The horse's head hung low, and he looked terrible. His feed was untouched. It was clear that he no longer had any energy.

"Hi there, boy," she said softly, holding out her hand for him to sniff. He shifted his weight away from her, and she moved closer. Immediately, Gallant Prince started. He threw his head up and bolted to the back of his stall.

Amy stood patiently, then tried moving a step closer once more. This time, the Thoroughbred flattened his ears and lunged at her with his teeth. Amy backed off hurriedly. Feeling frustrated, she let herself out of the stall. She stared at him as he eyed her, snorting nervously. After a few minutes, Amy lay back down in the stall next door, feeling helpless, her head heavy with tiredness.

❧

At seven o'clock, Lou appeared at the stall door with a mug of hot chocolate. "Did you get any sleep?" she asked, sounding concerned.

"Some. Not much," Amy admitted, taking a sip of the hot drink. "It got pretty cold, and Prince kept waking me up." She heard the door of Ty's pickup slam as he arrived for work.

He came right around to the barn. "How are you doing?" he asked. "And how's Prince?"

"I'm OK," said Amy, grinning weakly. "But Prince is still really stressed. He hardly rested at all during the night. And he still won't let me get near him."

Ty looked at Amy sympathetically. "You look like you've had a rough night, too," he commented.

Amy shrugged. "It was definitely the blackout that spooked him, but I'm wondering if he's worse when it's dark anyway," she said. "After all, the fire happened at night. Maybe we could try improving the lighting in the stall — like, try a different kind of bulb? Something with an orange glow might be really calming."

Ty looked thoughtful. "Well, OK. It's a start. I'll set it up while you're at school."

"Great," said Amy. "I'll make up a bran mash for him

and put some mint in it. That might tempt him to eat if he calms down long enough."

Amy tried not to think about how tired she was as she started on her usual chores of feeding all of the horses and cleaning stalls.

"Amy, I'll finish off the front stalls," Ben offered as soon as he arrived. "You look so tired already. And you need to get ready for school."

"Thanks, Ben, but I'm fine," Amy insisted, although she did feel weary. The last thing she wanted to do was spend the day stuck in classrooms, but she didn't have much choice.

"You're running late," Ben pointed out gently.

Amy looked at her watch in alarm. He was right. The time had flown by. She dashed into the farmhouse to get ready, making it to the bus stop with only seconds to spare.

❧

"Amy," said Soraya, looking concerned. "You don't look so good." She and Amy were sitting at one of the cafeteria tables during lunch. Amy's mind kept drifting off as tiredness overcame her.

"Well, neither would you if you'd been up half the night with a deranged horse," Amy answered, realizing that she hadn't brushed her hair that morning. She rarely spent a lot of time in front of the mirror before school, but today she hadn't even looked once. "Do you have a hairbrush with you?"

"Sure," said Soraya. She rummaged in her bag and fished one out. "So Prince is in a bad way, huh?" she asked.

"Yeah," Amy admitted. "He completely lost it. It was awful seeing him so worked up. All I could do was stare at first."

"I'm not surprised," said Soraya with feeling. "I'd have been scared, too. I'm really impressed that you stayed out there all night with him."

"I couldn't leave him," Amy said simply. She sighed, then frowned as she saw Ashley Grant making her way over to them. For once, she wasn't with Matt. Amy wondered briefly if Matt might prove to be a good influence on her, but as Ashley came closer, the stuck-up expression on her face made it clear that wasn't the case.

"Hello, Amy," said Ashley, flicking her hair over her shoulder. "How are things at Heartland?"

"Fine, thank you," responded Amy coolly, wondering what Ashley wanted. She had to want *something*.

"Really? I understand you've been creating a few problems for yourself. It's not surprising, I suppose."

"What are you talking about?" Amy demanded.

Ashley smirked. "A racehorse is totally different from one of your nice little trail ponies, you know," she said in a superior tone. "What makes you think you know what to do? I mean, you barely even go to the races. When did I last see *you* at Belmont Park?"

Amy glared at Ashley. She hated to rise to Ashley's bait — it just wasn't worth it. "I have better things to do than discuss that with you, Ashley," she said coldly.

"Well, you're looking a little rough around the edges, Amy. Maybe you should get yourself some sleeping pills. You and Gallant Prince could share them," Ashley purred. Then she turned on her heel and sauntered off.

"She is too much," Amy muttered.

"But how does she know you're having trouble?" asked Soraya, outraged. "Prince only arrived yesterday."

"Well, it was in the papers on Saturday." Amy hesitated. But Soraya was right. It was as though Ashley had known exactly what had happened last night. They looked at each other. The thought dawned on both of them at the same time.

"Matt," they said together.

Amy felt stung. She couldn't help it. It was hardly surprising that Matt knew — after all, he was Scott's brother, but even so . . . "How *could* he!" she exclaimed.

"He probably didn't think there was anything secret about it," said Soraya, trying to be fair. "The whole thing's big news. And I bet Ashley interrogated him anyway."

"But he must have known she'd leap on it like a vulture," Amy protested.

"He likes her," said Soraya. "And I guess that means he trusts her."

Amy groaned. It seemed incredible. As far as she was concerned, Ashley Grant was bad news.

"Amy! Come and check this out!" Ty called as Amy headed up the aisle of the back barn that afternoon. Ty and Jack Bartlett were bent over something on the ground.

Amy hurried over. "What are you doing?" she asked curiously. Grandpa was fiddling with some metal clips on an old car battery.

"It's all set," Jack said, straightening up and smiling. "I'm heading in — I want to get dinner on in time so I don't miss Monday night football on TV. Ty can explain it all to you, Amy."

"OK. Thanks, Grandpa," said Amy as Jack headed out of the barn. "So what's going on?" she asked, turning to Ty and gesturing at the battery.

"It's a backup system, in case we have another power outage," Ty explained. "Jack's set up a relay switch, just for Prince's stall. The car battery will power the bulb until the main power comes back on."

"What a great idea," said Amy.

"And we've put in an orange bulb," Ty continued. "I think you're right — it'll make a difference in the feel of his stall, too."

"How has he been today?" Amy asked. She looked over the half door at Prince, who stayed at the back of his stall. "Did he eat any of the mash I made this morning?"

"Some," said Ty. "But he left most of it. He's been incredibly jumpy, but at least he hasn't done anything crazy."

Amy looked at the stallion's dull coat. She could see his ribs. He obviously wasn't eating enough, and until he calmed down, he wasn't likely to, either. She sighed. "We need to figure out what it is that really spooks him," she said.

"I'd be surprised if it's something in particular," said Ty. "He's in such a state, anything sudden or different would trigger him."

"Do you think so?" mused Amy. "It would make sense if he gets worse when it's dark — I mean, the fire was at night. If that's true, we could try Rock Rose Remedy — that's supposed to soothe nighttime fears."

"I guess so," said Ty slowly. "But he's not exactly chilled out in daylight, either."

Amy turned to the half door again and leaned over it, studying the stallion. Prince started at her movement, then began pacing around, nervously eyeing Amy and Ty.

"Even us standing here talking seems to upset him," said Amy. "He's just so tense. The Walnut Remedy should help with that, though — and we could add some Crab Apple Remedy to help him cope with his injuries. But they're not going to be enough on their own. It seems like we could do everything in the book and it wouldn't break through his barrier. We need to make some sort of contact with him. We ought to try T-touch."

Ty nodded. "I've thought about that, too — only whenever I try to get near him, he breaks into a sweat and shies away."

"Well, this is only his second day here. He still needs to settle in," said Amy. "We'll just have to keep trying. I'll come back later. Right now, I need to do some work with Daybreak before it gets dark."

Amy couldn't be sure, but at the mention of Daybreak, a hint of irritation seemed to flit across Ty's face.

"Ben had her out earlier," he said.

"Oh," said Amy. "Well, I'll take her on a quick walk. She can handle a couple of sessions a day."

Ty shrugged. "I don't really think it's necessary."

"The more handling she gets, the better," said Amy, feeling slightly defensive. "I'll just work with her for fifteen minutes. Then I'll start mixing the feeds."

❧

Seeing the bright-eyed little filly was a pleasure for Amy after all the difficulties with Gallant Prince. She felt her heart warm as Daybreak's muzzle butted her affectionately. Amy led her out into the yard and went through the usual routine. As she ran her hand down the back of each leg, Daybreak knew what to do and lifted her hoof almost without being asked. Amy finished the session with a few moments of T-touch massage, working over the foal's body in light circles with her fingers. Daybreak stood still, loving the attention.

"She's looking great," said Ty, giving Amy a grin as he passed by.

"She's getting there," Amy agreed, smiling back.

Dusk was falling by the time Amy put Daybreak back into her stall. Her mind turned back to the stallion. She went to find Ty, who was already mixing the evening feeds. "I think maybe I should try some T-touch with Prince now, before it gets any darker," she said. "It'll be completely dark if I wait till after the feeds."

"That's true," he agreed. "I'll come and watch in case you need a hand with him."

They headed into the barn, where Prince was still pacing anxiously around his stall. He threw his head up and snorted as Amy carefully drew back the bolt and let herself in.

"Steady, boy," she murmured softly. He stood still at the back of the stall and stared at her. She could see how tense he was. Ty was right, he was ready to spring into panic for the slightest reason. She stepped closer, keeping up a steady murmur in a soothing voice. Prince backed away from her, shaking his head. Amy positioned herself in line with his shoulder so he could see her without feeling threatened, and moved closer again. Prince snorted and rolled his eyes at her, but he was right in the corner of the stall and couldn't go back any farther. Slowly, Amy took one more step and raised her arm to touch his neck.

At that moment, Ben came into the barn, the big door banging shut behind him. The stallion winced as though he'd been shot. He whinnied wildly and reared up, then plunged past Amy blindly, knocking her to the back of the stall.

"Amy!" Ty cried, shooting back the bolt of the door. "Get out!"

But now Prince was between Amy and the door. She was trapped behind him, and Ty had to hurriedly ram the bolt shut again to prevent the stallion from escaping. Prince whinnied again and turned around on his haunches. Amy pressed herself up against the back of the stall, her heart pounding.

"Amy!" called Ty desperately. "Climb over the side!"

Amy quickly sized up the side of the stall. There

weren't any toeholds, and the concrete blocks reached shoulder height. Then there were wooden slats above that. Even if she could manage it, her scrambling up would only distress Prince more. Panic began to rise inside her.

"I — can't," she stammered as Prince gave another piercing whinny, then snaked his neck menacingly in her direction. Acting instinctively, she threw her hands in the air. The movement startled Prince all over again. He leaped back, and Amy dived for the half door as the stallion reared again. Ty reacted instantly, letting her out, then banging the door shut behind her. She leaned against it for a few seconds, gasping for breath as Prince continued to thrash furiously around his stall.

"Amy, are you OK?" asked Ben, his face ashen.

Amy nodded. "I just feel awful for startling him again," she said.

"You did exactly the right thing!" exclaimed Ty. "You had to do something or you would still be in there."

"But we've *got* to calm him," said Amy. "Or he'll injure himself again."

"Was there anything that worked last night?" Ben asked in a low voice.

Amy shook her head in despair as Ty tried calling to Prince in a low, soothing voice. It had no effect. The stallion reared and kicked, letting out painful, high-pitched whinnies and crashing around the confined space of the stall. Then he stopped, staring at the three faces at his stall door but without appearing to really see them. His eyes were still glazed with panic. He stood still, his legs splayed, his nostrils flaring.

"So much for the orange bulb," Ty muttered.

"And so much for trying T-touch," said Amy shakily. "But he *was* calmer earlier. The bulb might have made some difference. Maybe there was something about the sound of the door that reminded him of the fire." But deep down, she knew she was clutching at straws. He had panicked for no real reason.

"We're going to have to leave him," said Ty. "You can't stay out here with him every night, Amy. When he loses it, there's nothing you can do — you can't get in there with him. Look what just happened."

Amy nodded miserably. She hated seeing a horse in such a state of distress. It seemed wrong to leave him on his own, but Ty was right. There was nothing anyone could do when Prince began to panic. At least, nothing they knew about yet. Deep down, Amy refused to believe that any horse could be completely beyond human reach. There *had* to be a way of communicating with him. And it was her job to find it.

Chapter Five

It was Wednesday evening, and Amy had just come home from school. Every night since Sunday, Prince had continued to wreck his stall after nightfall. As he'd settled into his new surroundings, he'd been slightly calmer during daylight, but Ty and Ben were still finding it impossible to groom him or lead him out.

"I think the only answer is joining up," said Amy.

Ty looked dubious. "I'm not sure it's safe to let him loose in the training ring," he warned. "He's so unpredictable."

"But we can't do any close work with him, like T-touch," Amy pointed out. "And he needs to get some exercise. At least with join up we don't need to work too close. The whole point is to keep him at a distance until he *chooses* to join up. You could come and watch out for me. I think it's worth a try."

Join up was usually the first step in building a solid relationship with a horse. It was a technique that Amy had learned from her mother, and so far she had never known it to fail.

"I still think it's too soon," said Ty. "It's bound to take a few days for the remedies to start working. Maybe we should wait until he's calmer."

Amy thought of being in the training ring on her own with Prince. Despite his injuries, he was still a powerful horse, and Ty was right — even though it wasn't like being trapped in the stall with him, it could be dangerous. But then she thought of Spartan, a horse she had worked with last year. Join up had worked with him, and he'd been almost as unmanageable as Prince.

"It might help us make a connection," said Amy.

"I guess you're right," Ty agreed reluctantly. "Do you want to try it now?"

"Why not?" said Amy. "We've still got an hour or so of daylight."

"OK," said Ty slightly wearily. "You know, Amy, we're going to have to treat the geldings, too. The stress is getting to them. Pirate and Red are feeling it the most. We can turn them out for part of the day, which should help, but they still have to come in at night. I'll talk to

Ben about using Walnut Remedy. That'll help them adjust to the change. And maybe some Aspen Remedy, to even out their nerves."

Amy looked at him seriously and swallowed. Ty was right. Prince's frenzied outbursts were bound to affect the other horses. She knew that Ben didn't want to say anything, but it was easy to tell from his face how anxious he was getting about Red. And Prince's behavior was the last thing Pirate needed. He already had a habit of pacing in his stall, a sure sign of anxiety and stress. Prince was definitely making him worse.

"OK," she said. "I'll do some T-touch with Pirate after we work with Prince." She gave a worried frown. By the time she'd tried join up, there wouldn't be much time for Pirate. But she told herself Prince had to be her priority — didn't he?

Amy headed to her bedroom to change. As she pulled on her jeans, Lou knocked on the door.

"Amy?" she asked. "Can I come in?"

"Sure," Amy said.

Lou stood in the doorway, a worried expression on her face. "Has Grandpa said anything to you about Gallant Prince?" she asked.

"No. Why would he?" Amy said, feeling a sudden rush of concern.

Lou sighed. "Well, he came in this afternoon complaining that he'd never seen such a barnful of jittery horses."

Amy took a deep breath and nodded, thinking of her conversation with Ty. She knew Grandpa was right.

"I just thought I'd let you know," said Lou. "I think he's getting worried, Amy. It's not like Grandpa to make comments like that."

Amy nodded. It was true — Grandpa usually didn't interfere in their work with the horses. He trusted Amy totally. If he was saying things like that to Lou, he *must* be worried. But they had to keep on going, for the time being. "Thanks for telling me, Lou," said Amy. "But we're just getting started. Maybe things will improve after we try joining up."

On the way down to the main training ring, Prince fought constantly, pulling backward and tossing his head as Ty gripped the reins tightly under his chin. Ty's face was grim, and Amy could read his thoughts — he didn't think this was a good idea. But they made it, and Amy opened the gate.

"We'll need to knot the reins so he doesn't trip," said Amy. "I'll do that if you can just hold on to him for a minute longer."

Quickly, Amy fixed the reins so they rested safely halfway up the stallion's neck. Then Ty let Prince go and walked back to the fence while Amy took her position in the middle of the ring. She unfurled the longline in her hand and flicked it gently in Prince's direction.

Prince started violently and reared before heading to the outside of the ring. There he stopped, staring at Amy, his nostrils flaring. She moved toward him and flicked the line again. Prince set off around the outside of the ring. It was the first time that Amy and Ty had seen Prince moving freely in the open since his arrival. At a trot, the stiffness in his right foreleg was easier to see. His head nodded and his right shoulder dropped slightly with each step — the limp that he would never entirely lose.

Amy squared her shoulders to the stallion's and kept driving him on. By doing this, she was showing him that he would have to keep on working until he chose to trust her. He circled the ring countless times before starting to tire. But although Prince was clearly reluctant to keep moving, the subtle signals that indicated the start of a join up weren't happening, either. He wasn't flicking his inside ear toward her or beginning to relax. He wasn't saying he wanted to stop and be with her. In fact, he still shied away every time she flicked the longline in his direction, and he rolled his eyes ominously. He seemed determined to stay as far from her as possible, and Amy noticed that his limp was becoming more pronounced the longer she kept him trotting around.

"Ty, I'm going to have to stop," she called, letting her shoulders sag. She looked the stallion in the eye and he snorted, clearly exhausted but defiant. "We're just not getting anywhere."

Ty jumped down from the fence where he'd been sitting to watch and approached Prince cautiously. Amy helped him corner the tired stallion and grab the reins. She shook her head. "It's as if he just won't respond. It's not that he can't — it's more like he *won't*. I just can't reach him."

That night, Amy lay in her bed and stared at the ceiling. Join up had worked with so many horses over the past months — Promise, Gypsy, Spartan. . . . Prince was the first horse that had chosen to stay on his own, at the outside of the ring.

Amy couldn't help but think of Spartan, the horse they had been rescuing on the day of her mother's fatal accident. When the tree had crashed onto the pickup truck and trailer, both Amy and Spartan had been injured. Amy thought back to the afternoon several weeks after the accident when, in a torrential thunderstorm, she had pursued Spartan around and around the ring, venting all her own feelings of anger and loss, until he had given her the signals she had barely expected to see. After that first join up, he had transformed into a gentle and loving horse again. Amy was the only one who had been able to reach him, because she understood exactly what he had been through.

Amy's thoughts drifted back to Prince. She remembered the pain and defiance in his eyes. She imagined once more the horror of the fire, the desperation to break free. But she could only *imagine* it. She couldn't *feel* it. Prince was still alone in his terror and his suffering. Perhaps he needed someone who truly understood, the way Amy had understood Spartan. Could there be anyone who might? There was his stable hand — the one who'd left the farm. Maybe he could help. Gradually, Amy began to drift off to sleep. Anything was worth a try. . . .

"Lou!" Amy called up the stairs the next morning just before she left for the bus stop. "What are you doing on Saturday?"

"I've got a meeting with a rep about new bedding for the stalls," Lou called back. "But that's all."

"Where?" asked Amy. "Near here?"

"No, it's up toward Hagerstown. Why?"

Amy thought quickly. "I was just wondering. Would you mind going a bit farther, across toward Baltimore? I want to go to Brookland Ridge to talk to that stable hand about Prince — the one who came with him. It's not much farther."

Lou appeared at the top of the stairs. She shrugged. "I guess so. It's only another half hour or so. If you really think it'll help."

"Who knows?" Amy admitted. "I'm running out of ideas."

✌

"Walnut, Rock Rose, and Crab Apple," Amy muttered to herself in the feed room on Friday night. "Rescue Remedy." She looked along the line of brown glass bottles, considering each one, then turned away. At this stage, it was probably more important to let the remedies they were already using with Prince take effect rather than trying new ones. They had to be patient.

But being patient was difficult. Earlier that evening as she was walking Pirate up to the smaller training ring to lunge him, Amy had passed Ben in the main ring, riding Red. As always, they made a striking pair, and she stopped briefly to watch. Ben sat tall in the saddle as he cantered Red in a circle. Red was fighting for his head, snatching at the reins, and Ben looked pale and tense as he encouraged the horse to settle into his stride and accept the bit. Red's neck was lathering up under the reins, until finally Ben slowed him to a trot. He spotted Amy and came over to the fence.

"He's not doing so well," Amy commented.

"No," said Ben, frowning. "He's just really wound up. I can't get him to concentrate."

"What's the problem?" Amy asked before she could stop herself.

"He's just being difficult generally," said Ben. He hesitated. "Ever since, well, you know —" He stopped and looked away.

Amy felt awkward. She knew what he meant. *Ever since Prince arrived.*

"Maybe you could try some diluted lavender oil with him later," she said quickly. "It might help. Just put some on your fingers and let him sniff it. If he likes it, rub it in gently under his forelock."

"OK," said Ben, turning Red back toward the center of the ring. "I'll give it a try. Thanks, Amy."

Amy wasn't sure Ben should be thanking her, especially when the root of Red's problems was so obvious.

Amy was relieved when Saturday finally arrived and there was something positive she could do about Gallant Prince. After an early lunch, she and Lou set off toward Baltimore.

"I said I'd be there by three-thirty," said Lou as she

drove down the driveway. "I'll take you to Brookland Ridge first. We should have plenty of time."

"Who is it you're meeting exactly?" asked Amy, realizing she hadn't paid much attention to Lou's plans.

"It's a company called Champions. They produce high-quality bedding. They responded to that flier I sent around," said Lou, "and they want to talk to me about the deal I suggested."

"Really?" Amy frowned. "I've never heard of them."

"I think they're new to the area," Lou said.

"So what makes this bedding special?" Amy asked, trying to be positive. She still wasn't sure about Lou's publicity idea.

"It's called SupaDri, and they say it's really light and absorbent," said Lou. "Of course we need to see whether it's as good as they say it is before we go any further. I was going to get some samples to bring back to show you. We don't need any *more* bad publicity."

Amy shot her sister a glance. It wasn't like Lou to be pessimistic.

"Well, as long as none of the horses develop allergies to it, I'm sure it will be fine. Besides, Prince isn't bringing us bad publicity yet," she added defensively. But she felt a pang of anxiety anyway. She *had* to find a way to help Prince, for everyone's sake.

✨

Lou dropped Amy at the entrance to the training farm. The words BROOKLAND RIDGE were worked into an impressive-looking wrought iron gateway.

"This will probably take me at least an hour," said Lou. "But my cell phone's on, so give me a call if you finish early." Amy waved and set off up the crisp gravel driveway. She reached the first barn and looked around. It was quite a sight. The barn was charred and blackened, and there was a big gap in the main roof where it had collapsed in the heat of the fire. It felt empty and desolate. No horses looked out over half doors, and there was none of the usual stable-yard bustle. There was still a lingering smell of burned wood, and the sound of sawing and hammering came from inside one of the stalls.

Amy hurried on to another barn that lay through an archway. Here, the stalls all looked as though they were in use. At one end, a stable hand was sluicing down the yard with a hose, while another swept the water into a drain. Horses pricked their ears and watched her over their stall doors as she walked across the yard to speak to the hands.

"Hi," she greeted them. "I'm looking for Sam."

One of them nodded toward the next block of stalls. "He's grooming," he said.

"Thanks," said Amy, heading toward the stall he'd indicated.

Inside, Amy found Sam grooming a big gray mare. He was whistling through his teeth as he worked and didn't hear her approach.

"Hi, Sam," she said over the half door. Sam looked up, startled. "Remember me? I'm Amy Fleming, from Heartland." She hesitated before continuing. "I was wondering if you could help me with something."

Sam gave her a friendly smile, but it soon faded as Amy explained how things were going with Prince. "I was wondering if it might be worth talking to his old stable hand," Amy finished. "The one who left."

"Ryan?" Sam looked guarded.

"Yes. Do you still see him?" Amy asked.

Sam shook his head. "Nope. None of us do."

"Why not?" Amy probed gently.

Sam looked at her seriously. "You don't have any idea what happened, do you?" he asked curiously.

"No," Amy admitted. "How could I?"

"Look, Ryan's in a bad way." Sam sighed. "He was badly burned in the fire, and he got blamed for what happened."

"Oh, I see." Amy looked thoughtful for a moment. "Just how badly burned?" she asked.

"Really bad," Sam replied. "He was blinded in one eye."

Amy was horrified. "Blinded," she murmured in surprise, staring at Sam.

Sam nodded. "I know," he said. "It's awful. We were all pretty shocked."

"And you say he got blamed, too?"

"Yeah," said Sam awkwardly. "He was the one on duty the night of the fire, and some people think it was his fault. The stable manager asked him to leave, so we all kind of think it's best to steer clear."

Amy didn't know what to say. She watched Sam as he bent down to brush the mare's legs. "But he was close to Prince?" she asked eventually.

"Very close," said Sam. "They were kind of inseparable. Ryan even exercised Prince sometimes."

That was all Amy needed to hear. "Listen, Sam," she said urgently. "I understand that you can't get involved, but could you at least tell me how to get in touch with Ryan?"

Sam straightened up. Amy's eyes pleaded with him. "Well, I can't see what harm that would do," he said. "I'll get you his address."

Walking back down the driveway, Amy thought about what she'd learned. Ryan had been there on the night of the fire, and he had been really close to Prince. She wondered if he would be able to help the stallion in some way. She pulled her cell phone out of her pocket to call Lou.

"I'm not far away," said Lou. "I'll be there in about twenty minutes."

As she waited at the end of the driveway, Amy studied Ryan's address. Sam had said the house was nearby.

"Do you think we could go there now?" Amy asked Lou once she was back in the car. "It'll save us another trip later."

Lou looked at her watch. "Sure," she agreed. "As long as you don't take too long."

The house wasn't difficult to find. It looked a little run-down. The paint was flaking off the window frames, and weeds were growing around the doorway.

Amy took a deep breath. "I'll be as quick as I can," she assured Lou as she stepped out of the car.

Amy rang the front doorbell and waited. There was no reply. She rang again. She could see Lou watching her, and shrugged. Still no one came to the door. Amy decided to give up and was walking back toward the car when she saw a girl hurrying toward the house, carrying several bags of groceries. She looked only a few years older than Amy herself — nineteen at most. Fishing in her bag for her keys, she stared at Amy suspiciously.

As she headed for the door, Amy turned and approached her. "Hi," she said nervously. "I'm looking for Ryan Bailey. Does he live here?"

The girl inserted a key in the lock and glanced quickly at Amy. "Why?" she asked warily. "Who are you?"

"My name's Amy Fleming. I'd like to talk to him about Gallant Prince."

"Well, if you're from the papers, I have nothing to say," said the girl. "And neither does he."

"I'm not," Amy said patiently. "I'm trying to help Gallant Prince. He's had a tough time. I guess Ryan's been through a lot, too." She smiled warmly and saw the girl's suspicious expression relax a little.

"So where *are* you from?" the girl asked.

"A farm called Heartland," Amy told her. "We work with horses that are injured or emotionally traumatized, like Prince."

The girl studied Amy's face. "Well," she said, after a pause. "I'm Beth, Ryan's wife. Why don't you come in?" Balancing her bags, she pushed open the door and tilted her head to indicate that Amy should walk in.

Amy followed her down the hall into a living room and stood waiting while Beth disappeared with the grocery bags.

"Please sit down," Beth said as she hurried back into the room, which was small but very neat. Amy sat on the sofa, and Beth sat opposite her in a wooden rocking chair.

"So how much do you know about what happened?" Beth began, fixing Amy with a curious gaze.

"Not much," Amy confessed. "I was thinking that

Ryan could help me piece it together. I spoke to Sam, one of the stable hands at Brookland Ridge. He gave me your address."

"Sam? How is he?" Beth asked.

"You know him?" said Amy, surprised.

Beth nodded. "I used to work at Brookland, too. So what did he tell you?"

"Well, just that Ryan was burned very badly in the fire," said Amy. "That he's blind in one eye. That he lost his job. And that he was really close to Prince."

Beth shrugged and nodded. "That's all true," she said. "So — what do you want?"

"Well." Amy took a deep breath. "I was hoping I could talk to him. About Prince. The horse is totally unmanageable, and we just can't seem to reach him. I thought maybe — he could tell me more about what Prince was like . . . before."

Beth stared at Amy and said nothing.

Amy began to feel uncomfortable. "Is Ryan here?" she asked uncertainly.

"He's upstairs." Beth sighed. "But he won't agree to see you. Or anyone else for that matter."

"Why not?" Amy persisted gently.

Beth took a deep breath. "He's just shut himself away," she said. "I gave up my job at the stables to look after him but . . ." she trailed off, her voice beginning to quaver. "Things have changed a lot. We were only married last summer. Everything was wonderful — we were really happy. Then the fire happened. . . ." Her voice broke again, and she drew another deep breath to steady herself. "The horses used to be everything to him. And Prince. What he and Prince had was really special, but now he can't do anything. I'm working at Kmart to make ends meet, but Ryan . . ."

She stopped and met Amy's gaze with tears in her eyes. Amy felt a rush of sympathy for her. Beth wasn't much older than she was, but she was already having to deal with so much — to carry so much pain and responsibility. It reminded Amy of the darker, difficult time she'd had in the weeks after her mother's death.

"I'm so sorry," she said quietly.

"I just wish —" Beth began, blinking back her tears. "I just wish I could get through to him. It's like I've lost him — like he's just not there anymore."

"But he's recovered from his injuries?" Amy asked.

"More or less," said Beth. "He's lost the sight in one eye, but he can still see fine with the other. His burns are pretty much healed. That's not the real problem anymore."

Amy hesitated. "Do you think I could try speaking to him?"

Beth looked doubtful. "You know, he really won't —" she began, and stared into the distance.

Amy waited. She thought about Gallant Prince and his pain and the idea that Ryan would understand that pain better than anyone. *Please,* she thought, *give me a chance.*

"Well," Beth said eventually, "I guess you can try."

Chapter Six

Beth poured a mug of coffee to take up to Ryan, then led Amy upstairs. She knocked softly on one of the doors. "Ryan?" she called.

There was no answer.

"Ryan," Beth repeated, "there's someone here to see you."

There was still no answer. Amy stepped forward and put her hand on the door handle.

"May I?" she asked. Beth hesitated and then nodded. She handed Amy the mug of coffee, and Amy opened the door.

Inside, the room was dark. The blinds were down, and it took Amy's eyes a couple of minutes to adjust.

"Ryan?" she said tentatively. A hunched figure was

sitting on a chair near a bed. "Ryan, my name's Amy. I've come to talk to you about Gallant Prince."

Ryan stared at her blankly. It was hard to make out his features, but Amy could see some scarring on the left side of his face.

"Can we open the blinds a little?" Amy asked. She moved toward the window, but before she could touch the blinds, Ryan spoke.

"Don't," he said, his voice low but urgent. "Don't touch them."

Amy stepped back from the window. "Oh, OK," she said. She stopped and thought for a moment. "I've brought you some coffee. Where do you want me to put it?"

Ryan didn't answer. Amy placed the mug on the dresser near him, then sat on the edge of the bed. Ryan turned away from her slightly.

"It must be really hard for you to think about Prince, Ryan," Amy began tentatively. "You were pretty close to him, weren't you?"

Ryan shifted in his chair but said nothing.

"He's so unhappy, Ryan," Amy went on. "He's been sent to my family's horse farm because we try to understand horses and help them through different problems. But I can't reach him. None of us can reach him. We're trying, but — it's like he doesn't want to be reached."

Ryan turned his back to Amy completely. The silence hung heavy in the air. Amy hunted for something to say.

"You know, it's weird that you're sitting here in the dark," she said, the words spilling out in a nervous rush. "For Prince, it's the other way around. It's the dark that upsets him."

She thought she saw Ryan flinch slightly at this, but it was difficult to tell in the dim light. Then he shrugged. "There's nothing worth seeing anymore," he said in a voice that was barely above a whisper.

Amy stared at him and swallowed. There was so much misery in his one simple sentence. "Ryan, that's not true," she said after a pause. "For one thing, there's Prince."

Ryan simply shook his head.

"I — I was wondering if you'd consider coming to see him," Amy said eventually. "I think he might respond to someone he trusts."

Ryan turned toward Amy and stared at her with his one good eye. "Someone he *trusts*?" he echoed, his voice harsh and challenging. "What makes you think Prince would respond to me?"

"I don't — I don't know anything for sure," Amy admitted. She sighed. There was another awkward pause, and Amy looked around the room as she searched for the right words. Her gaze landed on a pair of short riding boots, sitting neatly on the floor in the corner. A flash of hope ran through her. *He hasn't thrown them away,* she thought. Quickly, she scanned the room to see if there was anything else. On the back of the door, half hidden by a coat, she spotted a halter. She turned back to Ryan.

"Is that one of Prince's old halters?" she asked gently.

For an instant, Ryan dropped his guard. A look of contentment crossed his face. But then he masked it quickly.

"It's from before," he said abruptly. He shot Amy an angry glare, then turned away from her again.

"You know, Ryan, sometimes a horse can only be reached by the person who shares his pain. I know that's true. It's happened to me," she finished quietly.

Ryan shrugged. "It wouldn't help," he said coldly.

Amy opened her mouth to protest but stopped. Ryan didn't *want* to hear what she was saying.

"I won't see Prince again," Ryan said finally. "Now just go." A note of pleading had entered his voice. Amy realized there was nothing more she could do.

❦

Back downstairs, Amy found Beth in the kitchen, chopping vegetables. She looked up expectantly as Amy joined her.

Amy didn't know what to say. "Thanks for letting me try," she offered.

Beth nodded speechlessly, and Amy could see that she

was close to tears again. She searched Beth's face, realizing how hard the older girl was fighting to hold everything together and how little she had to fall back on.

"If you think of anything I can do to help —" Amy began.

Beth shook her head. "He's so determined to block out the past," she whispered. "I don't think anyone can make him face it." She put down her chopping knife and smiled sadly. "I'll show you out."

At the door, Amy reached for Beth's hand and squeezed it briefly, then turned and walked out to the car.

Briefly, Amy told Lou what had happened, then lapsed into silence as she thought over what she'd seen. She was filled with sadness for Ryan. It must be so hard for Beth, too, to see him buried in his world of pain. It was strange how neither Prince nor Ryan wanted to be reached. She thought of Beth's words: *He's so determined to block out the past.* It was as though he and Prince were both stuck, unable to look either forward or back. They were locked at the same point.

"I don't know what we can do about Prince now, Lou," she said slowly. "I was really hoping that Ryan would agree to come and help us work with him. I thought maybe he'd be able to get through to Prince, because they were together in the fire."

Lou looked at her in concern. "Isn't there anything else you can do?" she asked.

Amy sighed. "Well, I guess it's a question of time. Eventually, maybe . . ." She trailed off as Lou turned onto the freeway. "Anyway, thanks for taking me, Lou," she said. "I'll look at those bedding samples when we get back."

Lou smiled. "The bedding can wait," she said. "Prince is our priority now."

✌

As soon as Lou and Amy reached Heartland, Amy went looking for Ty. She found him in Gypsy's stall, in the front barn. He'd just finished grooming her and was putting the mane comb back into its bucket.

"So how did it go?" he asked her. "Did you have any luck?"

"Well — I met Ryan," said Amy.

"Ryan? He's Prince's old stable hand, right?"

Amy nodded. "It's so sad, Ty. He was half-blinded in the fire," she said. "And he's miserable. He's just shut himself away from the world. I thought it might help if he came to see Prince, but he says he won't. He doesn't want to do anything anymore."

Ty frowned thoughtfully. "Well, it was worth a try," he said.

Amy shrugged helplessly. "How has Prince been today?"

"Pretty much the same," said Ty. "Tense, restless. He snaps at me when I go anywhere near him."

"And the others?"

"Pirate's improving. The Aspen Remedy seems to be doing him some good. I'm not so sure about Red, though. The others are mostly OK."

"All right." Amy nodded. "Well, I guess I'll go and exercise Sundance," she said. "I haven't spent much time with him lately." Turning to go, she glanced at Ty.

He was looking at her, a strange expression in his eyes. "He's not the only one," he said.

"What do you mean?" asked Amy.

"Amy, we need to talk," said Ty. "About what happened. You know, at the Christmas party. I almost feel like you've been avoiding it."

"Avoiding it?" Amy exclaimed, feeling suddenly awkward. "That's not true. I just —"

"You just — what?" Ty prompted, his green eyes searching her face intently.

Amy looked away, hunting for the right words. "I haven't known what to say," she murmured eventually. It was true. She'd never had to deal with anything like this before. With Matt, she'd known she didn't want to be anything more than friends. But this was something different.

As she was thinking, Ty took a step closer.

"Ty," Amy said hurriedly. "I just don't want anything to change."

Ty stepped back. "OK," he said, looking hurt.

Amy felt more confused than ever. "Ty! No — I didn't mean —" she began. "I just meant that I'd hate to lose you — ever. And if things change between us, it could ruin everything . . . if . . . if —"

"If things didn't work out," Ty finished for her.

Amy nodded. "I guess," she said uncertainly. She took a deep breath and bit her lip. "I think I need more time to think about this. Can we talk some more later?"

Ty studied her face and gave her a slight smile. "OK," he said slowly, picking up the grooming bucket. "I'm not going anywhere."

"Well, it's certainly absorbent," said Amy. It was Sunday morning, and Amy and Grandpa were out in the storeroom with Lou, examining the SupaDri bedding that Lou had brought back from Champions. The thick sawdust-like flakes had soaked up nearly a quart of water. "And it'll be a lot less dusty than straw, which is good. Some horses have problems with the dustiness of straw," Amy added.

Lou looked pleased. "I'll tell them we'll go for it, then," she said. "There's a one-month trial, then they'll send a photographer to take some pictures of Heartland for the brochure."

"Well done, Lou," said Grandpa. "I think you've made a pretty good deal."

They headed out onto the sunlit yard, where Ty was sweeping up. "Actually, there's something else I want to ask you about," said Lou. "I might as well mention it now, since we're all here."

Ty stopped sweeping and propped the broom up against the wall. He faced Lou with a curious, expectant look.

"Go on," said Grandpa.

"I've been thinking we need some kind of weekly meeting," Lou announced, "where we sit down and talk about how all the horses are doing and anything else that's going on. Like a staff meeting."

"We all just tell one another anyway, don't we?" said Amy, puzzled.

"Well — sort of," Lou agreed. "But with everyone getting so busy, we don't always manage to do it soon enough. And that can lead to problems. Like when I sent Swallow back to his owner before he was ready."

Amy grimaced. That had been pretty embarrassing, and dangerous, too. Swallow had been unsafe to ride on the roads, and sending him home early was a nearly disastrous misunderstanding.

"I think it's a good idea, Lou," said Grandpa, and Ty nodded.

"It sounds a little too formal to me," said Amy.

"It wouldn't have to be," Lou said. "We could do it

over supper, one evening a week. Like, Wednesday evenings or something."

"OK," Amy agreed tentatively. "Would you like me to tell Ben?"

"Sure, that would be great," said Lou, hurrying off as the phone began to ring inside the farmhouse. "Thanks."

"I'll mention it to him," said Ty, picking up his broom again. "I was going to ask him to help me this afternoon. I think we should start lunging Prince."

"*Lunging* him!" Amy exclaimed. She thought of the struggle they'd had getting him down to the training ring only a few days before.

"He's not getting any exercise," Ty pointed out. "And we can't just turn him out with the others. He's a stallion."

"But, Ty, we don't know if we can control him." She looked quickly at Grandpa, who was listening intently.

"It's going to get more and more difficult if we don't exercise him," said Ty patiently. "He's a racehorse. He's used to intensive exercise, and not getting any at all is making everything else ten times worse. I *was* going to ask Ben to help," he added. "I think with the two of us, we should be fine."

Amy realized he was right. Stuck in his stall, Prince was only going to get more wound up. She nodded slowly. "Well, I guess," she said reluctantly. "What do you think, Grandpa?"

Jack looked thoughtful. "I don't like the thought of any of you being at risk," he said with a worried frown. "But it does sound as though you don't have much choice."

"We'll be careful," said Ty. "I promise."

❧

Later that afternoon, Amy decided to take Gypsy out for a ride on the trails. The mare had been cured of bucking so she would soon be returning to her owners, but Amy wanted to keep riding her to make sure she maintained her new good behavior. She mounted Gypsy and set off up the trail toward Clairdale Ridge.

As she passed the training ring, she was surprised to see Ty on his own, with Prince on the end of a lunge line. The stallion was trotting around, but he looked wild-eyed and resistant, his head held high. *Where's Ben?* she wondered, stopping Gypsy for a moment.

It was the wrong thing to do. The stallion immediately spotted the mare and let out a high-pitched whinny. Gypsy jumped and started sidestepping. Amy tried to calm her as Ty moved quickly to shorten Gallant Prince's lunge line and grab his bridle. But his sudden movement startled the volatile stallion. When Ty was only a step away, Prince reared up, his hooves flashing. Ty was taken by surprise. He dodged out of the way but lost his footing as the stallion's hooves rose again above him, striking out only inches from his head.

"No!" Amy gasped. Urging Gypsy to the edge of the training ring, she dismounted, looped the mare's reins over the fence, and leaped into the ring. Ty had managed to scramble to his feet, but as Amy approached, Prince snaked his neck at her and let out a piercing stallion's scream. Once more, Ty lunged for his bridle, and Amy moved in as fast as she could on the other side of Prince's head. They both managed to hang on as Prince tried to rear again. It took all their strength to maintain their hold as he pulled backward, fighting them, trying to shake them loose, while Gypsy whinnied excitedly from the fence.

Amy felt her grip loosening. Prince was too strong for them! Then, to her relief, she saw Ben out of the corner of her eye, running up the track. "Take Gypsy away!" she screamed.

Hurriedly, Ben freed Gypsy's reins and led her up to the stable yard. After a few more minutes of struggling, Amy and Ty at last managed to get Prince under control.

Amy's breathing was shaky and her knees were trembling. She turned to look at Ty. "You're bleeding!" she exclaimed, catching sight of a patch of blood on his shirtsleeve.

"I think he clipped my arm with his hoof," said Ty. "It's nothing serious. Let's get him back to his stall."

"So why wasn't Ben helping you?" Amy demanded between gritted teeth as they struggled to the barn. Prince was still prancing, agitated, and constantly trying to rear.

"Ben helped me get him down to the ring. Prince didn't seem too bad once he was trotting around, so Ben just ran back to the barn to get his gloves. I said he should wear them if he wanted to lunge Prince."

Amy nodded in agreement, noting the sting of ripped skin on her palms. When they finally reached Prince's stall, Ty quickly undid the straps of his bridle and let him loose as Ben appeared at the barn door, looking mortified.

"I should never have left you alone with him, Ty!" Ben lamented.

"It's not your fault," said Ty.

"Still, I should have already been wearing my gloves," said Ben. "Is your arm OK?"

"You need to clean it up and put a bandage on it," Amy insisted. "Are your shots up to date?"

"Yeah, I had one last month," said Ty. "But you're right, it does need some attention. I'll go to the house."

Together, Ty and Amy went into the kitchen and told Lou what had happened. She went to get the first aid kit, and Ty rolled up his sleeve. The cut wasn't deep, but there would be bruising.

"Lou, if Grandpa finds out about this, he might make

us send Prince back," Amy said as she gently patted Ty's arm with some cotton.

Lou hesitated. "We can't hide something like this from him, Amy. And you can't blame him for feeling worried. He cares about you and Ty — and he hates seeing anyone put at risk. That's all."

"That's more or less what he said this morning," Ty agreed.

The three looked at one another, feeling dismayed. Suddenly, Amy stood up and started sifting through the papers by the phone. "I don't care what Ryan says," she said. "I know deep down that he can help Prince. I'm sure he hasn't blocked him out completely. He still has Prince's halter hanging on his door. I'm going to call him."

She found Ryan's number and picked up the phone.

"Beth?" said Amy. "It's Amy, from Heartland. Could you ask Ryan to come to the phone?" she continued. "Please. Tell him we really need his help." She quickly explained what had happened with Prince and listened as Beth said she would try.

Amy waited patiently, hoping Ryan would come to the phone. After what seemed like forever, she heard Beth's voice again.

"He won't come," she said. "I've begged him, but he just won't."

Amy felt her heart sink. "There's nothing else you can do to persuade him?" she pleaded.

"I'm sorry, Amy," said Beth, her voice breaking. "I wish he'd listen. Not just to me. To anyone."

"OK," said Amy more gently. "Thanks for trying, Beth."

Amy hung up the phone and sat back down at the kitchen table.

"We just have to keep on working Prince," said Ty. "There's nothing more we can do."

Lou took a deep breath. "I don't know how long we can keep going, though," she said. "Especially when Grandpa finds out about this afternoon."

Amy looked at her sister pleadingly. "Do we have to tell him, Lou?" she asked. "Can't we give it a few more days? At least the remedies will have more time to work."

Lou looked from Amy to Ty and back again. "Well —" she said. "OK. I won't say anything — yet. But if there's no improvement soon, we'll have to let him know."

❧

At school the next day, Amy told Soraya about Ty's near miss with Prince.

"I just keep seeing Prince's hooves flying toward Ty," said Amy, her face pale. "It was my fault. I shouldn't have taken Gypsy past the training ring. That was what triggered it. If anything serious had happened to Ty . . ." She trailed off.

Soraya's eyes searched Amy's, full of concern. "Amy, I know Ty's kind of special to you."

Amy looked at her friend quickly. "It's not that, it's —" she stuttered and stopped.

"Is there something you want to tell me?" Soraya probed.

Amy blushed slightly, her thoughts in turmoil. "No! Well — I mean — I don't really know." She looked at her friend honestly. "Promise you won't say anything to anyone."

"Of course!" breathed Soraya.

"Well, we kissed on Christmas Eve — at the Grants' party."

"Amy!" Soraya exclaimed. "How have you kept *that* quiet? I would have been telling everyone."

Amy grinned sheepishly, then her smile faded. "Soraya, Ty's always been my friend. I'm terrified of losing him. What if things went wrong? It's bad enough the way things are with Matt."

"What are you talking about? Things aren't that bad with Matt," said Soraya reassuringly.

"Oh, no? When did he last hang out with us? We haven't seen him for ages — not since he started dating Ashley."

"Well, I guess that's what happens when you're dating

someone," said Soraya. "You spend a lot of time with them. It's kind of sweet, in a way."

"*Sweet?*" said Amy in disgust. So much had changed in her life in the last year — she'd lost her mother, then Pegasus, and it didn't help when a good friend like Matt disappeared, too. What if she and Ty ended up more distant, instead of closer? Amy felt cold inside at the thought. Ty was really important to her. But then she pulled herself together. "Anyway, promise you won't tell anyone about Ty," she finished.

Soraya nodded. "I promise. I won't say a word."

Chapter Seven

Lou put extra effort into making supper special on Wednesday evening. As Amy came in from the stables, the comforting aroma of chicken pot pie greeted her.

"Smells great!" said Ben, coming in behind her. "Hey, maybe we should have a meeting every night if the food's going to be this good!"

Lou grinned at him. "Yeah, right," she said. "Like I'd get any work done if we did that!"

Soon Jack, Ben, Amy, and Ty were sitting at the table. Lou took her seat at the end, with a pile of papers next to her.

"I've created a file for each horse," she said as she began slicing and serving the pie. "We can jot down notes about how they're doing, then I can type up the details later. Maybe we could offer a report for owners as part of our service. What do you think?"

"Why not? Sounds good," said Jack with a smile. "This is all very organized, Lou. Are the horses in any particular order?" he teased.

"Alphabetical, of course," said Lou. Then she grinned. "Only joking," she added hurriedly.

In between bites of Lou's delicious pot pie, they discussed the horses. At the top of the list, of course, was Prince.

"There's not a lot we can say at this stage," Amy said honestly, shooting Ty a nervous glance. They still hadn't told Grandpa what had happened on Sunday afternoon.

"Has there been any progress at all?" Jack asked.

"Well — no. Not exactly," said Amy.

"So do you think you're going to get anywhere with him or not?" Lou questioned.

Amy thought quickly. It went against everything in her to admit defeat. She took a deep breath.

"Yes, I'm sure we can make a difference," she said firmly. "But it's still very early. He needs more time."

"The problem is, he's unpredictable," said Ty. "And it's too early to say what effect the remedies are having."

Grandpa looked around the table at everyone's solemn faces. He took a deep breath and let it out in a sigh.

"Whatever we do, it's going to take time," said Amy

hastily, before he could speak. "Prince is too badly damaged to be cured in just a couple of weeks."

"Amy, the issue isn't just Prince," Grandpa said quietly. "I know he's important, but you have to think of the other horses, too. And your own safety. I'm aware of how dangerous he is. Your mother would never have risked herself and everything else at Heartland for the sake of one horse."

Amy's eyes met Grandpa's gaze. She knew he was right. He smiled gently, but his eyes were serious. "And, that's not all. We need to let Luke Norton know if we're wasting our time," he concluded.

There was a brief silence as everyone let his words sink in. Then Lou stood up. "Seconds, anyone?" she asked, opening the oven door. The brief interruption seemed to break the heavy mood.

"Yes, please," said Ben, holding out his plate. "This is my kind of food."

Lou cut into the new pie. "At least Gypsy's doing well," Ben commented as Lou handed his plate back to him.

"She is, isn't she?" Amy agreed. "She hasn't bucked for weeks."

"Do you think she's ready to go, then?" asked Lou.

Ben and Amy exchanged glances, then both nodded. "I'd say so," said Ben.

"Good," said Lou. "What about Melody and Daybreak? Daybreak's doing OK, isn't she?"

"Yes," said Amy slowly. "But she's still pretty feisty. She could use a couple more weeks. I want to be sure she'll respond well to a new owner."

To Amy's surprise, Ty spoke up. "She'll always be feisty," he said, shaking his head. "That's just her personality. I think she's ready to go now."

"Ty!" Amy protested. "You know how difficult she was before."

"Sure," said Ty. "And I know how good she is now. It would be good for her new owner to get to know her at this stage."

"But she's not ready yet," Amy insisted. She frowned at Ty. He looked away.

They fell into silence again.

"She's always good with me when I handle her," Ben said reasonably, after a minute or two. "I haven't had any problems with her for a while now."

Lou looked at Amy inquiringly. Amy stared at her plate and said nothing.

"Amy," said Ty quietly, "you want to keep Daybreak because you have a bond with her. I know she's special to you. You don't want to lose her."

"That's not true!" said Amy, but with less conviction.

"I think it is," said Ty, challenging her with his gaze. "You said you don't want anything to change," he added significantly. "Well, you know, Amy, sometimes things have to change, whether you like it or not." There was a long pause. "It's time for **Daybreak** to move on."

Amy's cheeks flushed **an angry** red. She glared at Ty. The atmosphere suddenly felt very charged.

Lou turned to Ben. "Do you agree with Ty, Ben?" she asked hesitantly.

"I think I do," said Ben, looking slightly embarrassed. "They're both ready to go."

"All right," said Lou firmly. "Well, tomorrow we should start looking for a new owner for them both."

Amy sat in silence for a few minutes, avoiding everyone's gaze. She felt humiliated. She couldn't believe that Ty had disagreed with her like that, and in front of everyone else, too. *Especially* turning her own words against her.

By the time they had finished their dinner meeting, it was long past nine o'clock. Ben and Ty headed home, and Amy helped Lou clear away the dinner things. Then she slipped out into the yard and went to Melody and Daybreak's stall. Melody was standing up, dozing. She barely shifted as Amy let herself quietly into the stall. Daybreak was curled up on the straw, but she instinctively scrambled to her feet at the sound of the bolt.

"Hi, there," said Amy, holding out her hand to the

filly. Daybreak snorted eagerly, her eyes shining brightly in the dim light of the stall. Amy knelt down and put her arms around Daybreak's neck.

"I don't want you to go, baby," she whispered, feeling a lump in her throat. Daybreak nudged her curiously, and Amy stroked her tufty mane. Ty's words flashed through her mind again: *Things have to change, whether you like it or not.* But who was he to say that to her? He wasn't the one who'd had his whole life turned upside down! Maybe if he had, he'd understand how difficult it was to keep losing the things she loved.

Amy's mind turned to Ryan, sitting in the darkness on his own, trying to cope with the loss of so much — his life at the stables, the sight in his eye, and Prince. She thought of his burns and his scars. For a moment, she felt ashamed of herself. At least she was still fit and well. But she *had* lost a lot, and she'd had to move on. Surely she could help Ryan see that whatever happened, there was always a new beginning? He needed to regain his trust in life and find something to hope for. He had to face his past and face up to meeting Prince again.

Amy's thoughts went back to Spartan. She hadn't given up on him. She'd kept on and on until he realized that it was better to trust her than stay on his own with his fear and pain. As she smoothed Daybreak's silky neck, Amy suddenly realized that she couldn't give up on Ryan, either. She kissed the filly's nose and got to her feet.

"See you in the morning, girl," she said, letting herself out. She hurried over to the back barn and made her way to Prince's stall where as usual, he paced around restlessly. He started as she approached, snorting nervously.

Amy leaned over the half door and fixed his rolling eyes with her gaze. "I'm not giving up on you, boy," she said softly. Prince stood still in the middle of his stall, his muscles tense, ready to leap back. Amy spoke to him determinedly. "I'm going to bring Ryan to you if it's the last thing I do."

Amy got up early the next morning, feeling more optimistic than she'd felt for days. She headed out to the barns and got right to work, determined that things would go well. When Ty walked into the barn, she managed to greet him with a smile.

"I've already fed the geldings," she told him. "I'm just about to start the feeds for the front stalls."

"I guess I'll start mucking out then," Ty said in a slightly guarded tone. He hesitated. "Amy — I'm sorry. About last night."

Amy made herself look at him. "I'm sorry, too," she

said. "And, Ty . . . about — you know. Can we talk?" She smiled again, more easily this time.

Ty looked surprised. "Well — I guess. Yeah. Of course."

Amy looked at her watch. "But maybe not right now. We've got seventeen horses to deal with."

"Yeah," Ty grinned, obviously relieved. "Well, later then."

❧

As usual, the morning turned into a scramble to make the bus on time. After sweeping the yard, Amy realized she only had ten minutes to shower and change. She dashed inside and leaped up the stairs. Nine minutes later, she was tearing back down again.

"Bye, Lou! I'm leaving!" Amy called. She grabbed her coat from where she'd left it on the back of one of the chairs.

"See you," she heard Lou reply. Then, when Amy was halfway out the door, she heard Lou's voice again. "Oh, Amy!"

"Lou, I gotta go!"

"Wait — there's a package for you."

Amy stopped and stuck her head back around the door. "A *package*?"

"Here — take it with you!" said Lou, hastily stuffing it into Amy's outstretched hand.

❧

"Open it!" Soraya cried when Amy showed her the brown package on the bus.

"I will, I will," Amy said. "Just hang on a minute."

"It looks like a book," said Soraya.

"No, it's too light," Amy told her. She started to tear off the layers of tape. "Feels more like a video." She opened one end and peered inside. "Yep," she said, frowning in puzzlement. "Definitely a video."

As she finished unwrapping the package, a note fell out.

"*Dear Amy,*" it read. "*I found this the other day when I was cleaning out the office. I don't know if it'll help, but you had asked about Ryan and Prince. This just about says it all. Sam.*"

"Who's Sam?" queried Soraya, who hadn't been able to resist reading over Amy's shoulder.

"A stable hand at Brookland Ridge," Amy said slowly. "The one I went to see about Ryan."

"Oh, right," said Soraya. "So what did he send you? Is there a label on it?"

Amy opened the case, but the video didn't have any details. "Nothing besides the note," she said, still feeling puzzled. "I'll just have to wait till I get home to watch it."

"All day? That's going to kill you!" Soraya teased.

❧

Soraya was right. It was impossible for Amy to concentrate. Even the sight of Matt and Ashley sitting together in class didn't bother her for once. All she could think about was what might be on that video. The moment she got home, Amy headed straight for the VCR, not even bothering to take off her coat. She pushed the video into the machine and pressed PLAY, sitting down on the edge of an armchair to watch.

At first she couldn't figure out why Sam had sent it. The first few minutes showed a couple of races from the previous season, taped from TV. But then, at the end of the second race, the screen went blank for a few seconds. When the tape resumed, a familiar face appeared — Ryan's. Amy leaned forward expectantly.

The difference between this Ryan and the one she'd met was unbelievable. On the video, his face was smooth and boyish, and there was a deep sparkle in his dark brown eyes. He spoke confidently into a microphone, a broad smile on his face.

"He knows what he's got to do," he was saying. "He's as ready as he's ever going to be."

"Can we quote you on that?" asked the interviewer, laughing.

"Yeah, yeah, I guess." Ryan laughed, too.

"So that's straight from Ryan Bailey, Gallant Prince's stable hand," the interviewer announced to the camera.

He turned to Ryan once more. "If you're that confident, you must have something on the race yourself?"

For a moment, Ryan's face became serious. He shook his head. "I would never gamble on Prince," he said. "You don't gamble on your friends. I just want him to run a good, safe race."

The camera moved in closer as he spoke, and Amy looked into Ryan's eyes. There was no mistaking the love and commitment in his words.

The picture cut to the race itself. Amy tried to imagine how Ryan must have felt, seeing Prince out there on the track, straining every sinew in his body to do his best. She willed the stallion to win. He did — by a full length and a half. Amy sighed as the scene changed once again, this time to the winners' enclosure, where Prince stood proudly, still looking bright-eyed and alert, barely winded from his run. Amy got out of her armchair and moved closer to the screen, scanning the busy scene for Ryan. Luke Norton was there, next to Prince, and another man she didn't recognize, but whom she guessed must be the owner. Then, at Prince's head, holding on to his bridle and praising him, Ryan appeared. As the camera panned around, Amy caught a fleeting glimpse of the stallion resting his nose on Ryan's shoulder and playfully chewing at his collar. Ryan's face was glowing.

Amy replayed the video, and there it was again, a pure moment between Ryan and Prince. There was no mistaking it. The camera moved away to pan over the crowds, then the video cut to another race. Amy stared for a moment, then turned the TV off. This video held the key to it all, she was sure of it. Again, she thought of Beth's words: *He's so determined to block out the past.* Amy was certain he wouldn't be able to block this out, if only she could persuade Ryan to watch it.

"Amy?" Ty's voice disturbed her thoughts.

"In here," Amy called, still staring at the blank screen.

Ty came in and looked at her, then at the TV, puzzled. "What are you doing?"

"Sam sent me a video," she said.

"Sam?" Ty frowned for a moment, then nodded. "Oh, yeah. The stable hand up at Brookland."

Amy waved her hand toward the TV. "The video is of Prince. I was just watching it."

"Was it helpful?" Ty asked.

Amy got up. "I don't know for sure," she said slowly. "But it gave me an idea. Were you looking for me?"

"Yeah." Ty gave her a slightly awkward look. "Lou's arranged for some people to come and see Melody and Daybreak. They should be arriving pretty soon. I thought you would want to know."

"You're kidding me! How could she have found someone already?" Amy cried, dismayed. She stared at Ty, all her feelings of uncertainty from the night before suddenly washing back over her.

"It does seem pretty sudden," Ty admitted. "Lou did some calling around during the day, and one couple said they wanted to come right over. But she had to go to the bank and the supermarket, so I said we'd handle it."

"Great!" snapped Amy. "I guess I'd better go get changed."

Chapter Eight

Once she was in her bedroom, Amy tried to calm herself down. *Melody and Daybreak have to go,* she reminded herself. *It's not going to be easy, however long it takes to find someone. Come on, Amy. Remember all the good things.* She took a deep breath and headed downstairs.

Out in the yard, Ty was already talking to a pleasant-looking couple who appeared to be in their early forties. Amy walked up to them.

"Hi, I'm Amy Fleming," she said politely.

"Pleased to meet you," said the man. "Jon Sleighman. And this is Carole, my wife."

Amy nodded and smiled. "Melody and Daybreak are in the front stalls here," she said. "We'll bring them out to you."

Working in silence, she and Ty quickly put halters on the horses and led them outside.

"Pretty foal," said Jon. "Nice-looking mare, too. Hey, girl." He stepped forward and offered Melody his hand to sniff. Carole approached Daybreak and did the same. Amy watched them carefully. They were clearly used to being around horses.

"Daybreak had some problems initially," she told them, explaining Daybreak's history. "We've been handling her really carefully so that she'll trust the person who trains her, when she's old enough."

"Oh, you don't need to worry about that. We aren't going to train her," laughed Carole. "Not for riding, anyway. We quit riding a few years back. We just want a big family farm, you know — goats and sheep, mainly. We used to have a couple of quarter horses, but we sold them when we gave up riding."

Ty and Amy exchanged glances.

"You're not going to train her?" Amy repeated.

Jon smiled reassuringly, seeing Amy's expression. "We miss having horses around the place," he explained. "So we decided to keep an eye out for any horses needing a loving home."

For a moment, Amy didn't know what to say. She looked down at Daybreak, who was nuzzling her pocket, and thought of the little foal's potential. She had

her whole life ahead of her. If she went to the Sleighmans' farm, it would be like retiring her before she'd
even begun, and she would forget everything she'd
learned. Quickly, Amy made up her mind. Avoiding Ty's
gaze, she said gently, "You know, Daybreak needs some
training. Like I said, she has a fiery personality. If she's
left to her own devices, she'll become unmanageable
pretty quickly."

"But she's the cutest little thing," Carole protested,
smiling.

"She's only like this because we work with her every
day," said Amy, feeling awkward. "We have a strict routine. She needs it."

Jon and Carole looked at each other. "Well —" Jon
hesitated, "we don't really want to get into all that."

Amy nodded and smiled apologetically. "In that case,
I don't think Melody and Daybreak are quite right for
you. I'm sorry."

Jon and Carole took in her words, looking uncertain.
Amy could see their disappointment, but she was sure
she'd made the right decision. She glanced at Ty but
couldn't read his expression. "We'll certainly keep you
in mind when we have horses that are more suitable,"
Amy offered.

Carole looked pleased. "OK," she said. "We'd appreciate that." The couple patted Melody and Daybreak.
"Mind if we look around before we go?"

🙠

As the Sleighmans drove away, Amy began to feel anxious. Ty hadn't said much during the visit, and as the couple had said their good-byes he'd hurried back into the barn. What if he thought she was just trying to stop Daybreak from leaving? She'd have to set him straight.

"So, did you think I was wrong?" she inquired, looking into the stall where he was grooming Melody.

Ty stopped and looked at her. "Of course not," he replied. "They weren't right for Daybreak."

Amy felt relieved. She hesitated. "It was just that — last night —"

"Amy, you know I think Daybreak's ready to go, but . . ." Ty trailed off, seeming to hunt for words. He fiddled with the brush in his hands.

Amy nodded. "I know she is, too," she agreed. "You're right. I don't want her to leave, but she's ready."

"Still, I shouldn't have said what I did," Ty said deliberately, looking regretful.

Amy was surprised. She looked at him, her eyebrows raised.

Ty continued. "I mean — you know — the stuff about things having to change. That was sort of about something else. It just came out. I didn't mean it."

"I know, Ty." Amy felt suddenly nervous. It didn't make sense. She'd always been comfortable talking to

Ty. But this was different. She forced herself to look directly at him. "I know what it was about. I think I just — need some time," she said hesitantly.

Ty stopped his grooming and raised his head, looking deep into Amy's eyes.

Amy's heart was thumping and her stomach felt fluttery. She swallowed, and waited for Ty to say something. As she did, she heard the sound of Lou's car coming up the driveway.

"It's Lou," Amy said, looking at Ty with a relieved smile. She heard the car door slam. "I'd better tell her how it went with the Sleighmans," she said.

❧

Lou was disappointed with the news. "I guess I didn't ask the right questions on the phone," she said, dumping several bags of groceries onto the kitchen table.

"Well, they were very nice, but we do need someone who's going to work properly with Daybreak," Amy explained, putting cereal boxes away in the cupboard.

"I'll make that more clear from now on," said Lou. "Hey, what was in that package?" she asked.

"It was a video. Of Ryan and Prince, before the fire. Sam sent it."

"Really? Did he think it would help somehow?" Lou seemed puzzled.

Amy frowned thoughtfully. "I'm not sure. It might give Ryan a jolt — make him realize how badly he and Prince need each other — if I can just get him to watch it. He might not want to, but it's worth a try."

"So you'll need to make another trip?" Lou frowned. "I'm really busy on Saturday, Amy. I'm sorry, but I can't take you up there this weekend."

"That's OK," said Amy. "I'm sure I'll find someone to drive me."

When she'd finished helping Lou put the groceries away, Amy went back out to find Ty. He was just finishing up with Melody and was putting the grooming kit back into its box.

"Hey, Ty," she said tentatively, "you're off on Saturday, aren't you?"

Ty nodded. These days, he hardly ever took days off; there was always too much going on at Heartland. "Yeah, why?" he asked.

"What were you planning to do?" she asked. "You said you might go shopping or something."

Ty looked mystified. "Yeah, during the day. Then I'm catching up with a few friends later that night."

"Where are you going to do your shopping?" queried Amy.

"What is this? Some kind of test?" asked Ty good-humoredly.

Amy smiled. "No. It's just that I want to try to show that video to Ryan, and Lou's busy," she explained.

Ty grinned. "Ah, I see," he said. "Well, why don't I take you? I could pick up what I need in Baltimore."

"You read my mind," laughed Amy, feeling relieved. "But are you sure that's OK?"

"Of course it is," said Ty. "It might even be fun," he added teasingly.

Amy nodded. "That's perfect," she said. "I'll check with Beth to make sure she's not working."

❦

Later that evening, after supper, Amy went to the phone and punched in Ryan's number.

"Beth?" she said when Ryan's wife answered the phone. "It's Amy, from Heartland."

"Amy," Beth said flatly.

Amy thought she sounded tired and depressed. "How are you?" she asked gently.

Beth sighed and didn't answer the question. Instead, she said, "Listen, Amy. I know you want Ryan to visit Prince, but there's nothing I can do to persuade him. There just isn't. I tried really hard the last time you called."

Amy chose her words carefully. "Beth, I understand. I'm sorry to keep calling, but I really think Ryan and Prince need each other right now. I think they can help each other to come to terms with everything."

"I'm not so sure," said Beth. "Ryan doesn't want anything to do with horses."

Amy could hear the doubt in her voice and wished there was more she could say to convince her. "I have something that might change his mind," she said. "You told me that Ryan wants to block out the past. Well, Sam sent me a video of one of the races that Gallant Prince won last season. It shows Ryan and Prince together, like they used to be. Beth, they shared a special friendship. I think if Ryan could remember that, it would be something that would help. I think he'd want to see Prince, and it would do them both some good."

Beth was silent for a few moments. "I doubt he'll watch it," she said eventually. "But you're welcome to come over, if you want."

"Could I come on Saturday?" Amy asked. "Are you working?"

"Only in the morning," said Beth. "You could come in the afternoon, after two o'clock."

"Thanks," said Amy. "I'll see you then."

She put the phone down and went outside. Ben and Ty had gone home for the night, and everything was quiet in the front barn. She breathed in the cool air and walked up the path toward the turnout paddocks. She could see a few stars where the clouds had parted in the sky, and she gazed up at them, thinking. Last night's dinner meeting already seemed ages ago. She thought of Ty's words once more: *Sometimes things have to change.* He was right. She hoped she could show Ryan how to accept the past. Until he did, she felt sure he wouldn't be able to face the future.

It was drizzling when Ty and Amy set off toward Baltimore on Saturday. It felt odd to Amy, heading out of Heartland in Ty's pickup — nearly all the time they spent together was on the farm, with the horses. But it felt good, too. After a while, Ty put in a tape, and they drove along listening to it.

As they sped along the highway, Amy thought about the conversation they'd had after the Sleighmans' visit. She was still feeling confused — and a little guilty, she realized.

"Ty," she said hesitantly. "You do — understand, don't you?"

"Understand what?" asked Ty, glancing at her quickly.

"What I was saying. About — needing more time. We didn't really get to finish our conversation."

Ty looked thoughtful. "I think I understand," he said

slowly. He paused. "You're afraid things might not work out. Right?"

"Kind of," said Amy. "It's just that I don't want things to be weird between us. I don't know what I'd do if we weren't friends anymore. You really mean a lot to me."

It was quiet for a moment as Ty concentrated on changing lanes. After a moment he said, "I feel exactly the same way."

"You do?" asked Amy uncertainly.

"Yeah. I don't want to lose you, either, Amy," said Ty. He paused, then added softly, "The most important thing is that we're friends. Everything else can wait."

🙟

As they pulled up outside Ryan and Beth's house, the rain started coming down more heavily. Amy pulled her coat around her and got out of the car.

"See you later," she said to Ty, making a run through the rain for the front door.

Beth opened the door almost at once. "Hi," she said, looking uneasy. "So you've brought the video."

"That's right," said Amy.

Beth opened the door wider. "Well, come in. I'll take your coat, you must be soaking."

Amy sat down in the living room and pulled the video out of her bag while Beth fixed them each a hot drink.

"Which race is it?" called Beth. She sounded uncomfortable, and Amy wondered why.

"It's Pimlico," said Amy. "He won by a length and a half."

Beth brought in two mugs and nodded. "I know the one," she said. "The Maryland Breeders' Cup. Ryan was just so happy after that."

"Were you there?" asked Amy.

"Sure, I was there." She sat down on the seat opposite Amy. "I didn't get to go into the winners' circle, but I was really close, so it was almost as good." Beth gave a sad smile. "Can we watch it?" she asked softly.

"Of course, but I'd really like Ryan to see it, too," said Amy firmly. "That's why I'm here."

Beth shook her head, looking more uncomfortable. "It's like I said, Amy. I've told him about it," she said. "More than once. Why don't we just play it with the volume turned up a little?"

Beth looked miserable, and Amy didn't know what to say. If Beth had already asked Ryan, there was little she could do. But she *had* come a long way, and she was convinced that the video would make a difference. She wasn't going to give up so easily.

"Can I at least try talking to him again?" asked Amy determinedly.

"Well, I'll go and let him know that you're here," said

Beth. She went upstairs, and Amy heard her knocking on Ryan's door and speaking in a low voice. Amy waited. There was no response, and Beth came back looking upset.

"It's no use," she said. "To be honest, I think he's getting worse."

"Please let me try," begged Amy.

Beth shrugged. "I'd prefer if you didn't right now. I want to give him some time to think about it."

Beth was close to tears, her hands trembling. Watching her, Amy felt like Beth had little hope left.

"I'd really like to watch it anyway," said Beth, her voice cracking. "I — I'd like to remember the way things were."

Amy looked at her sympathetically. "You must miss the horses, too," she said. "Couldn't you go back and work at the training farm, once Ryan's better?"

Beth shook her head. "I can't go back there. It would make things too awkward. It doesn't matter so much for me. I'd only been there a couple of years. But for Ryan —"

"How long had he been there?" asked Amy.

"Since he was fourteen," Beth replied.

Amy nodded.

"It's good to talk about it," said Beth, giving Amy a grateful smile.

"Would you like to put the video in now?" Amy asked. Beth nodded eagerly. She slid the video out of the box and pushed it into the VCR.

❧

Beth smiled wistfully as Ryan's happy, boyish face grinned into the camera. She watched the screen intently.

"All the other grooms used to tease him," she told Amy. "He adored Prince like a . . . a . . . little brother."

As the camera moved in on Ryan's face, Amy heard a sudden sound. She looked around. Ryan was standing in the doorway. Beth followed Amy's gaze.

Amy's heart turned over when she saw the sad expression on Ryan's face. Slowly, he walked closer to the sofa, his good eye never leaving the screen. Amy slid over, and he lowered himself to sit down beside her. Beth, her face full of amazement, moved from the armchair.

"Ryan," she whispered, squeezing onto the end of the sofa next to him.

The three watched in silence for a few more minutes, until the video reached the end of the interview. As the old Ryan spoke, Amy turned around. She felt a tug of emotion as she saw Ryan sitting quietly. Beth had put her arms around him and was rocking him gently.

"It was all my fault," he said under his breath. "He'd still be racing if it weren't for me."

"Why do you say that?" asked Amy. "Sam said you got blamed because you were the one on duty — but I still don't see how it was your fault."

"It wasn't," said Beth softly, but Ryan hardly seemed to hear her.

"I ruined his life," he said, his voice full of anguish. He placed his hand on his forehead and closed his eyes.

"Ryan, wait, wait," Amy said urgently, throwing a bewildered look at Beth. "What happened?"

Ryan paused and looked up.

Amy met his gaze. "Tell me, please," she encouraged.

Ryan cleared his throat, then began to speak.

"I was on late duty. It was one of the stable rules, one of us always had to stay overnight. We had a rotation list. There's a special apartment — you don't have to sleep in the barn. Anyway, it was really cold in the stalls that night, so at the start of my shift I set up three kerosene heaters in the middle of the aisle. I thought they'd be safe. The horses couldn't reach them. But some of the kerosene must have leaked or something. And with everything so dry, the fire took over fast."

"Ryan, you know it wasn't just that," Beth broke in and turned to Amy. "After Ryan had gone up to the apartment, someone else came in and stacked the hay for the morning feeds right next to one of the heaters. It was one of the guys who was just about to go off duty. He must not have seen the heater. Even so, he shouldn't have left it there. It was really dumb. But he took off before the fire started, so Ryan got the blame."

"But it *was* me — *I* put the heaters out," insisted Ryan.

Amy listened intently. "What happened next?" she asked. "Prince broke loose?"

"His stall was closest to where the fire started, and the heat must have got intense pretty fast. He broke down his door," Ryan said, his voice breaking. "When I heard the wood cracking and the fierce whinnies, I tore out of the apartment. I ran in and Prince was the first thing I saw. I'll never forget that. He was wild with pain. I led him outside but then I just left him there. I can't believe I did that to him. I'll never be able to face him again."

"But didn't you go into the stables and bring out the other horses?" said Amy.

"Yes, he did," Beth interjected again. "That's how he lost the sight in his eye."

"I was on the last horse," said Ryan. "It was Masquerade. I'd freed all the others. By the time I got to his stall, his door was already on fire, and he was wild with panic. The bolt was hotter than a branding iron, but I managed to yank the door open. Then Masquerade just barged past me, and I fell. . . ." Ryan stopped, his throat drying up.

Beth finished the sentence for him, quietly. "He landed on a burning block of wood," she said.

The terrible image of the scene filled Amy with distress. She took a deep breath. "You can't keep blaming yourself, Ryan," she said gently. "You did everything you could for the horses. You put yourself in danger for them."

"But the fire was *my* fault," said Ryan.

"Ryan, you know it wasn't," Beth argued. "They just wanted someone to blame."

Ryan turned to Amy. "After it happened, I was in the hospital for about three weeks. When I was released, I knew there wouldn't be a job for me. How could they keep me on after what I'd done?" He gulped hard. "Now it's too late. I've ruined Prince. I've ruined everything." He put his head in his hands.

"You haven't ruined anything," Amy protested, desperate to reach him. "You saved all those horses. And Prince will be OK, but he needs you to recover. I know he does. I don't think there's any more we can do unless you come to see him. Nothing's ruined, Ryan. Prince can have a good life at stud — but only if he can get over his fear."

Ryan shook his head vehemently. "He won't forgive me," he said fiercely.

Amy felt overwhelmed with frustration. Ryan was still alive, and so was Prince. Why wasn't Ryan willing to face his past and try to help Prince recover? Amy thought of her mother and how much she ached to see her again. That wasn't going to happen, ever. But at least Ryan had the chance to start over.

She began to speak, the words tumbling out of her. "Ryan, Prince isn't blaming you," she said. "He's suffering, just like you. He can't get over what the fire did to him. He can't trust the world around him or the people in it. It's as if he's constantly on the edge of panic."

Ryan didn't say anything, but Amy could tell he was listening. She continued, feeling more and more confident as she spoke. "You've got to come through this together, Ryan. Prince needs someone who understands what he's been through. You can't shut yourself away here, feeling responsible for what happened. It's not fair to Beth, or you, or Prince. Don't you think you've punished yourself enough?"

Ryan stared at the floor and was silent. Amy waited, wondering if she'd said too much. But what else could she do? She *had* to convince him. "You know, I understand how you feel better than you think," she said in a quieter voice. She hesitated, then added, "Last year, my mom was killed in an accident. I had persuaded her to rescue an abandoned horse during a bad storm. We crashed on the way home. I — I blamed myself for what happened."

She saw Beth look at her, her face full of sympathy.

"I had to face up to Spartan, the horse we rescued," Amy continued quietly. "It wasn't easy. But in the end, I realized that we needed each other. As I worked with him, I managed to stop blaming myself."

Ryan listened, then nodded, slowly. He studied his hands, and eventually he spoke. "What — what does Prince look like now?" he asked.

Of course, Amy thought. *Ryan hasn't seen Prince since the night of the fire.*

"He has scars," she told him honestly. "But they're healing really well. He's unsound, and he's lost a lot of muscle because he's too stressed to eat much. But we can help him through all that."

Ryan nodded slowly. "But what if —" he began, then stopped.

"What if —?" Amy prompted gently.

"What if he doesn't recognize me?" Ryan asked hoarsely, his face in his hands.

Amy stared at Ryan, suddenly feeling the full force of how hard this was for him. She hunted for the right words. "Ryan, he'll recognize you," she said. "You're still the same person. He'll know your voice, he'll know your smell. He'll know it's you."

There was another long pause as Ryan considered her words. Beth took his hands and stroked them gently. "Amy's right, Ryan," she whispered.

Ryan looked up, and Amy saw the tears streaming down his face.

"OK," he said. "I'll come."

Chapter Nine

Amy reached out and touched Ryan's arm. "It'll be hard, I know, but I'm sure it's the right thing," she said. "Really sure." She heard a truck pull up outside and guessed it must be Ty. "Listen, I've got to go now." She stood, suddenly feeling exhausted.

Ryan looked up from the sofa and gave an anxious smile. "I'll see if I can take the bus over to you. When should I come?" he asked.

"Whenever you like," said Amy, smiling back. "But the sooner the better."

Ryan nodded. "OK," he promised quietly.

"I'll leave the video with you," Amy said. "You might want to watch it again. And I'll leave my address and phone number, too."

Amy quickly scribbled down the details of how to find Heartland and handed them to Beth, who got Amy's coat and walked her to the door. As Amy reached for the doorknob, Beth stepped forward and hugged her impulsively. "Thank you so much, Amy," she said.

Amy smiled at the older girl. "Beth, I'm happy I could help. You should thank Sam for sending the video."

"It was more than the video," Beth interrupted her warmly. "It was you, Amy. You believed in Ryan."

Amy realized she *had* believed in Ryan. As soon as she had seen the riding boots and halter in his room, she knew Ryan had something to live for. She also knew that a person could lose sight of what makes life worth living. "It's like I said," she explained. "I've had to deal with a lot myself. It's taken me a long time. And it'll probably be the same for Ryan. It'll be tough, but he's taken his first step."

Beth nodded slowly. "I know," she said. "It's OK if it takes a while. I just want him back."

Amy smiled again. "Thanks for trusting me," she said. Ducking out into the rain, she raced for Ty's pickup.

❧

"How did it go?" Ty asked immediately as Amy clambered in.

"Ryan's going to come to Heartland," she said as she

fumbled for her seat belt. Her mind flooded again with the image of Ryan's grief for Prince.

"Amy!" Ty exclaimed. "You're amazing." He studied Amy's face and saw the mix of emotions there. "It wasn't easy, was it?" he added.

"No," said Amy. "He's so — so damaged." She suddenly felt close to tears. "Just like Prince," she added.

"Hey," said Ty gently, touching her arm.

It was too much for Amy. She buried her face in her hands.

"Hey, Amy," said Ty again, and put his arm around her shoulder. Amy leaned against him and sobbed. She felt so awful for Ryan. And his pain brought back her own sorrow, too. After a few minutes, she pulled herself together and took a deep breath. She sat back in her seat and smiled at Ty gratefully through her tears.

"Thanks, Ty," she said with a sniff. "It's just —"

Ty smiled. "You don't have to say anything. I understand," he said. He handed her a tissue from his pocket. Amy blew her nose.

"I guess we'd better get going," she said, making an effort to be cheerful. "We can't leave Ben on his own for too long."

"Sure," said Ty, starting the engine. "So when's Ryan going to come? Did he say?"

Amy shook her head. "I think we have to leave that to him," she said. "He'll come when he's ready."

Ty nodded thoughtfully as he pulled out onto the road. "Well, let's hope he comes soon," he said. "Both for Prince's sake and his own."

Back at Heartland, Amy checked on Ben and the horses, then headed into the farmhouse. Grandpa was just finishing a mug of coffee and looked at Amy expectantly as she walked in.

"Guess what," Amy said immediately, with a smile. "Ryan's agreed to come and see Prince."

Grandpa smiled. "That's wonderful, Amy." He paused. "But do you really think it will help?"

Amy's smile faded. Grandpa's inquiring look made her realize that nothing was over yet. Ryan might have said he was coming to Heartland, but they couldn't be sure that it would make any real difference to Prince. She hesitated. "I don't know for certain, Grandpa. But I really think they need each other," she said honestly.

Jack looked at Amy with concern. "Amy, you're a fighter. Just like your mother. Though I'm not sure even she would have gone this far." He shook his head and gazed out the window. Then he pulled on his coat and headed for the door. "Well, I'm looking forward to meeting Ryan." He put his hand on the door handle and looked solemnly at Amy. "If he comes."

At these words, Amy felt herself go cold inside. "I'm sure he'll come, Grandpa," she said. But a voice of doubt nagged at her. Ryan might change his mind, and what would happen then?

Grandpa nodded. "I hope you're right, Amy," he said. "I really do."

The next morning, Ty and Amy stood at the door of Prince's stall, watching him snatch a few uneasy mouthfuls of hay from his hay net. "He's definitely getting thinner," Ty said worriedly. "He's just not eating enough."

Aware of their presence, Prince was restless, stamping a hind leg as though something was irritating him.

"Maybe I should try join up again," Amy suggested.

"Is that a good idea?" Ty said doubtfully. "Wouldn't it be better to wait and see what effect Ryan has?"

"We don't know when Ryan's going to show up," Amy pointed out. *If he comes.* A pang of anxiety went through her as she remembered Grandpa's words. "In the meantime, we need to try anything we can to connect with him."

"Well, OK," Ty agreed. "But you'll need help getting him to the training ring. You shouldn't try to manage him on your own."

"I know," said Amy. "Can you give me a hand?"

"Sure," Ty said. "Do you want to try now?"

Amy shrugged. "We might as well. Otherwise, I'll put it off all day. I'll go get his bridle."

She headed for the tack room, wondering if they were wasting their time. She hoped Ryan would come soon — but what if he didn't? There was still the awful possibility that he might change his mind. Who was she to think that two short visits from her could make such a difference?

Slinging a bridle over her shoulder, she headed back for the barn. She wouldn't allow herself to think about it. They'd have to wait and see.

"Come on, boy," she soothed as Prince shied away from her and Ty in his stall. They drew closer, and he threw his head up. Patiently, they held their ground and tried again. After a few attempts, they managed to clip a lead line to his halter. Amy held on to him as Ty fought with the stallion to put on his bridle. At last they led him, sweating and resistant, from his stall, and set off from the barn toward the turnout paddocks.

Once he was out in the open, Prince thrashed his head around and struck out with his foreleg. Suddenly, he stopped dead. Amy looked up at him, astonished. She held the reins more tightly in case he was about to rear. His ears were pricked and his nostrils flared quickly in and out. Every muscle in his body was quivering. Amy turned her head and followed his gaze.

🙟

In front of them, at the top of the path, was Ryan. He, too, was standing perfectly still, staring at Prince. He was wearing dark glasses, and his face was deathly pale. Prince craned his neck forward, still flaring his nostrils.

Ryan started to walk toward them, slowly extending his hand. "Prince?" he said in a voice that was barely above a whisper.

Prince gave a gentle nicker of recognition, and then he whinnied. As Ryan came closer, he jerked at the reins in Ty and Amy's hands. When Ryan was just a few feet away, Amy and Ty released Prince, and he jogged forward, his neck arched and his nose stretching toward Ryan.

Ryan's face split into a huge smile. "Hey there, fella!" he exclaimed as the stallion nuzzled him. Prince snorted in short, joyful bursts. Ryan buried his face in Prince's mane as if he wanted to convince himself it was all for real.

"I missed you, Mister Man," Amy heard Ryan say. Amy looked at Ty in wonder. *Could it really be as simple as this?*

Chapter Ten

After a moment, Amy came to her senses. Of course Prince couldn't be transformed that quickly. Ryan's visit wasn't a miracle cure, no matter how much she wanted it to be. Still, she felt hopeful as she watched Ryan and Prince together. Then she noticed that Prince's reins were hanging loose. Ryan wasn't holding on to them.

"Ryan," she started to say, trying to disguise her alarm so as not to frighten Prince. But she was too late. Just as she rushed forward, Ty's cell phone started ringing. The piercing sound panicked the sensitive horse. He shied violently and tossed up his head, catching Ryan unaware, jolting him hard and sending him staggering backward. Ryan's sunglasses fell to the ground and Gallant Prince reared above him. Amy flung herself at the horse, making a desperate lunge for his bridle. She missed, and the stallion plunged forward with a defiant whinny.

"No!" Amy cried, throwing herself at Prince again. This time, she caught hold of one of his reins. In seconds, Ty was there, grabbing hold of the bridle. Together, they fought to get the stallion under control.

"Prince! Prince, steady boy," Amy heard, and she suddenly realized that Ryan was with them, at Prince's head, looking into his eyes. Prince snorted, his nostrils flaring nervously, but the sound of Ryan's voice seemed to calm him down. He stopped struggling and stood, sweating, as Ryan reached out and stroked his face.

"Are you OK, Ryan?" Amy asked. Ryan looked pale and shocked, but he nodded.

Amy heaved a sigh of relief. "We'd better get Prince back inside," she said shakily.

Prince followed them quietly back into his stall. Amy and Ty stood outside the door as Ryan carefully took off Prince's bridle. Amy watched anxiously. Prince fidgeted and shook his head impatiently, but he didn't go crazy again. Ryan lifted the reins over his head, then stepped forward and handed Amy the bridle. He gave Ty a nervous nod, and Amy realized they hadn't been introduced.

"Ryan, this is Ty," she said. "We've both been working with Prince."

Ty smiled warmly at Ryan, and Ryan seemed to relax a little.

"Can I stay here in the stall with Prince for a while?" he asked.

Amy and Ty exchanged glances. Ty looked doubtful. "I'm not sure it's safe," he said. "What do you think, Amy?"

Amy studied the stallion. As Ryan talked to them over the half door, Prince walked up behind him and nudged him. Amy looked into the horse's eyes. Some of the fear and nervousness had gone — but Prince still eyed Amy and Ty warily. She hesitated.

"Please," said Ryan. He turned to face Prince and stroked his neck.

"Well —" Amy hesitated. "OK. But we'll be close by. If he starts acting up, all you have to do is call."

❧

"You've left them in the stall together?" Lou asked, looking shocked. After taking Ryan a grooming kit, Amy had hurried up to the farmhouse to tell Lou and Grandpa the news. Ty had stayed behind in case Ryan needed anything.

Amy nodded. "It felt like the right thing to do," she said. "And Ty's in the barn."

"But you've barely been able to handle this horse,"

Grandpa said, his face full of concern. "Do you really think it's a good idea?"

"I don't think Prince will get violent with Ryan in the stall," said Amy. "But I do think it's going to be a while before he accepts anyone else." Ryan's arrival was only the start — nothing was going to get better right away. "We'll give them a little longer. Then I'll see how they're doing."

"Well, I sure hope he's safe," said Lou cautiously. "Anyway, I was just coming to find you. I've had another phone call about Melody and Daybreak. A woman wants to see them. She called me on her cell phone. She's planning to drop by in the next hour."

"Oh, OK," said Amy. "Well, let me know when she arrives. I'm going back to the barn."

As Amy set foot outside again, she saw Ty heading toward the house. He motioned to her.

"What is it?" she called, breaking into a run. "Is Ryan OK?" she asked anxiously.

"Sort of," said Ty. "But I think he's having a rough time. You might want to reassure him."

Amy headed into the barn and made for Prince's stall. She looked over the half door. Ryan had a body brush in his hand and was holding on to Prince's halter. Prince looked tense and awkward, and Ryan was looking frustrated.

"Come on, Prince, boy," Ryan was muttering. He caught sight of Amy watching and turned to face her. "He just won't stand still," he said. "He never used to be like this. He used to stand like a rock. He's — he's so different. . . ." His face looked stricken.

Amy saw the doubt and confusion in Ryan's face as Prince pressed himself against the back of the stall, his body tense and unyielding.

"Ryan, you can't expect Prince to get better all at once," Amy said gently, letting herself into the stall. Prince immediately rolled the whites of his eyes and snorted warningly. Amy stood slightly behind Ryan. "Why don't you approach him?" Amy instructed. Ryan extended his hand to the horse. Prince hesitated, then slowly reached out his neck. Ryan took a step forward, and Prince allowed him to stroke his mane.

Amy let out her breath. "Ryan, if you weren't here, I wouldn't be able to stand in Prince's stall like this. It may not seem like much, but you *are* making a difference. Believe me, it's true."

Ryan shook his head. "I thought — I thought, after everything you'd said, that it would be easy," he said hoarsely. "I — I thought everything would be like it was before."

"Things are never going to be exactly the way they were," Amy told him gently. "You have to accept that. And so does Prince. But things can get better. And they can move forward. We can work with Prince together," she went on. "He already trusts you more than any of us, and Ty and I can show you other ways of reaching and reassuring him. Then, in time, other people will be able to handle him, too."

Ryan looked at her doubtfully. Amy looked back, challenging his gaze. "You have to want things to change. And you have to work at it," she said. "Nothing's going to get better unless you want it to."

Amy heard Lou calling her and guessed that Melody and Daybreak's prospective owner had arrived. "It's up to you, Ryan," she added as she let herself out of the stall. "It's really up to you."

Amy walked around to the front barn, her thoughts whirling. She could imagine how hard this must be for Ryan, but she was concerned at how easily defeated he seemed. Working together to heal Prince was going to be a long haul — if Ryan stuck with it at all. She hoped she had said the right thing — that Ryan wouldn't give up. She sighed and turned her thoughts to Melody and Daybreak.

A pickup was parked next to the empty barn, and a woman in her fifties was talking to Lou and Ty. She smiled as Amy walked up, and she held out her hand. "Jess Morgan. Nice to meet you."

"It's Ty and Amy you need to talk to," Lou was saying. "They'll tell you everything you need to know. I'll be in the farmhouse if you need me."

Jess smiled at them. "Well, I remember you, but I guess you probably don't recognize me," she said. Amy and Ty looked puzzled. "I came to your open house last October," Jess explained. "I was very impressed, and I learned a lot. Especially from that session with Lisa Stillman's Arabian."

"Well, thanks." Amy smiled. That was a good sign — Jess had not only come to the open house but had been interested in Heartland's techniques.

"Do you work with foals a lot?" Amy asked as she and Ty led Melody and Daybreak out into the yard.

"It's kind of becoming my speciality," Jess told her. "I run a small stable, and I have a couple of brood mares already. I've raised a handful of foals, but I'm learning all the time. You never stop doing that."

Jess gently ran her hand over Daybreak's body, then asked her to lift her feet, one at a time. "You've done a lot of the groundwork," she said as Daybreak willingly obliged.

"Yeah. It hasn't been easy, though," Amy admitted, explaining their early problems with the foal.

Jess listened intently. "Well, if you're happy for me to take them, I'll be calling you for advice," she said. "And

I'm not very far away. You can come and see how she's doing for yourself if you'd like."

Amy was touched. This was exactly what she wanted to hear. "We'd love for you to take them," she said, looking quickly at Ty for reassurance. He nodded, smiling. "And I'd love to visit them, too — when I have time!"

"Great!" said Jess. "But I won't be able to pick them up for a few days. My trailer is being fixed. Is that going to be a problem?"

"Not at all," said Amy. "Just give us a call."

"I will," Jess said. She shook Ty's hand firmly and then Amy's. "I think you're doing a great job here," she added as she pulled out her car keys. "Losing your mom must have been really hard. But I'm sure she'd have been proud of you. Real proud."

Yes, it was really hard, thought Amy as she walked back to the barn to check on Ryan. *But I haven't given up. I've never given up.* As she opened the barn door, Ryan was letting himself out of Prince's stall, carrying the grooming kit. She hurried over to him and searched his face as he handed it to her. He met her gaze frankly.

"Amy," he said. "I'm sorry about earlier. I've been thinking about what you said." He paused. "You were right — Prince does need me. He doesn't understand what's happened to him, so he's lost faith in everything, just like I did. But I won't give up. I'll work with Prince until he trusts me again."

Amy felt a wave of relief wash over her. Ryan was going to fight. "I'm glad," she said warmly. "And don't forget, you won't be working alone. Ty and I will do everything we can to help, too."

Ryan nodded. "I know," he said. "Thanks." He paused. "Is it OK if I come tomorrow?"

"Of course," Amy said. "You can come whenever you want."

"Great," Ryan smiled. "The bus trip's easy enough. See you tomorrow, Mister Man," Ryan said softly, reaching up to caress the horse's face. Then he turned and headed for the door. As he went, Prince watched, craning his neck over the stall door. Ryan closed the barn door behind him, and the stallion gave a shrill whinny of distress.

"It's OK, boy," Amy soothed. "He'll be coming back." But Prince ignored her and stood still, staring at the barn door. Gently, Amy reached up to stroke his neck, and he flinched, then snapped at her with his teeth. They were going to have to be patient. There was no way to know how long it would take before Prince began to accept her — or anyone else.

⸮

"You move your fingers in little circles," Amy explained. It was Thursday, and Amy had only been home from school a little while. Ryan had visited twice since Sunday, and Prince was improving steadily. As long as Ryan was there, Amy had been able to work with Prince herself. He would let her put on his halter and groom him as long as she did it fairly quickly. But he was still a long way from being really manageable. Whenever Ryan left him, he became distressed, and at night he was almost as restless as before.

Now Amy was standing next to Ryan, teaching him how to do T-touch. Carefully, he followed her instructions. His fingers were soon moving gently and rhythmically over Prince's skin.

"That's it," said Amy, watching him closely. As he worked, she could sense that the stallion was relaxing slightly. "I'll let you keep going now, on your own," she said. "He's still awfully restless with me here."

"OK," said Ryan. "I'll give it a try." He went back to work, a frown of concentration developing on his face. Amy backed out quietly and left Ryan to work with the horse on his own.

She hurried around to the front barn to help Ben with the evening feeds. Ty had taken the day off, and there was a lot for just two people to do.

"How's it going with Prince now that Ryan's here?"

Ben asked as they scooped chaff, beet, and alfafa into buckets.

Amy sighed. "Slowly," she replied, shoving one of the scoops back into a feed bin and replacing its lid. "But there's definitely a difference."

"How much longer do you think Prince is likely to stay?" Ben queried.

Amy looked at him quickly. Although Red had settled down, thanks to the Aspen Remedy and lavender oil they'd been giving him, he still wasn't really himself. As far as Ben was concerned, the sooner Prince went to stud, the better — but Amy knew he wouldn't dream of saying so directly.

"Well," she said. "Ryan is making good progress on his own. The problem is getting Prince to work with other people. That's what the owner's going to want. And that's going to take time." She frowned. "We're going to have to keep working with him while Ryan's around, then gradually build up the work we do with him when Ryan's not here. I think it's going to be several weeks before he's calm enough to go to stud."

Ben nodded. "So what will happen to Ryan once Prince has recovered?"

Amy wasn't sure what to say. She shrugged and picked up two of the feed buckets. "I don't know, Ben," she replied, heading for the door. "That's a tough one."

"He's going to be miserable if they're separated

again," Ben pointed out. "I know how I'd feel if I was separated from Red — and we haven't been through half as much."

Amy stopped and turned as the truth of Ben's words hit her. In her determination to make a breakthrough with Prince, she hadn't thought of what would happen in the long run. She'd brought Ryan and Prince back together, and now they were both facing the past, little by little. But as Prince improved, the time would rapidly approach when he would have to go to the owner's stud farm, leaving Ryan behind. Once again, Ryan would be left with nothing: no Prince, no job, no future.

Amy swallowed. Had she found a cure for Prince — but only at Ryan's expense?

Chapter Eleven

"I think we should keep this picture up," said Amy, pointing at the photo of her mother on Pegasus. "All the others can come down. What do you think?" It was Saturday morning, and Amy was in the tack room. She had asked Grandpa and Lou to come and look at her ideas for rearranging it.

"That's fine by me," said Grandpa. "I'm sure we can find room for the others around the house."

Lou nodded. "I've been checking on the prices of racks," she said. "They're not too expensive. How many do we need? Another six?"

Amy looked at the expanse of wall and nodded. "Yeah. Six should fit. That'll make a big difference."

"That's no problem. I'll order them on Monday," said Lou.

Ty stuck his head around the tack room door. "Whoa, it's crowded in here," he said cheerfully. "Can you pass me Prince's bridle — and that long line."

"Prince's bridle?" Jack queried.

"Ryan's ready to start some lunging work with him," Ty explained. "Ben and I are going to help him, though, just in case. Amy and I talked it over last night."

"Well, that's definitely progress," said Jack, looking pleased. "Has anyone told Luke Norton how things are going?"

Amy exchanged glances with Ty and shook her head. "No," she admitted. "To be honest, I've been putting it off. I think Ryan should have as long as possible with Prince before he goes to stud. It's going to be hard on him to lose him again."

Ty nodded in agreement. "It's not going to be easy."

Grandpa stroked his chin and looked thoughtful. "Well, we have to contact Luke Norton soon," he said. "We said we'd keep him posted on how things were going. We can't keep Prince here any longer than we absolutely need to. You know that. He's caused a lot of disruption, and things still aren't back to normal, even now that he's improving."

Amy nodded, miserably. Grandpa was right. However they looked at it, Prince was going to have to go. The faster he regained his trust in the world, the sooner Ryan was going to lose him.

"But we do need to plan things out carefully," Grandpa continued. "Let's contact Luke Norton today to say there's been an improvement, and that's all we need to say at the moment. Still, Ryan's going to have to come to terms with him going to stud sometime soon. I can't really see any way out of that."

Amy sighed. At least they weren't going to rush into anything, and maybe some other solution would occur to her in the meantime. "Thank you, Grandpa," she said. "I'll go and call Luke now. And I'll get a box for the rest of these pictures."

❧

Amy went indoors and found Prince's file. Quickly, she punched in the telephone number for Brookland Ridge, feeling nervous when she heard the ringing.

"Hello?" she said when someone picked up the phone. "Could I speak to Mr. Norton, please? This is Amy Fleming, from Heartland."

"Speaking," said Luke Norton. "Amy. Good to hear from you. How are things?"

"Well — we have some good news," she said. "Prince has been improving steadily over the last week or so. He's much calmer, and we've started lunging him."

"Really?" Luke sounded astonished. "Well, Mr. Hartley will be pleased to hear that. He's been saying he wants to come and see your setup and find out what you're up to."

"Oh, he has?" said Amy, taken aback. "When was he thinking of coming?"

"I can't say exactly," Luke said. "He'll probably just drop by when he's down your way. I'll give him the green light, OK?"

"Yes, that would be fine," Amy stammered. "We'll be expecting him."

She put the phone down slowly, realizing she had to talk to Ryan. It wasn't fair to keep this from him. He needed to start to prepare himself for being parted from Prince. She took an empty box to the tack room and, working fast, cleared the wall of pictures and ribbons, then headed up the path to see how Ty and Ryan were doing with the lunging.

Prince was trotting around the edge of the training ring with Ryan in the center. His head nodded when his injured leg touched the ground, but apart from that, he looked reasonably relaxed. As she approached, Amy was struck by the change in Ryan. He looked assured and confident, a very different Ryan from the figure she'd first seen hunched in his darkened room. Ty and Ben watched from the edge of the ring as the horse responded to Ryan's commands.

"He's doing well," Amy said, going to stand alongside Ty.

Ty nodded. "How was your talk with Luke Norton?"

Amy was about to tell him when she realized that Ryan had overheard Ty's words. He brought Prince to a halt and led him over.

"What's this about Luke Norton?" Ryan asked anxiously.

Amy looked at Ryan frankly. "Mr. Hartley wants to come and see how Prince is doing, Ryan."

"Already?" he whispered.

Amy nodded. "Did you get along OK with him?" Amy asked.

"Well, I don't think Mr. Hartley had anything against me before the fire," said Ryan. "I don't know how he felt about that. It was Luke Norton who told me I was out of a job." He looked at Amy miserably. "Well, if Mr. Hartley's coming here, I guess that means Prince'll be going to stud soon?"

Amy nodded unhappily. "That's pretty likely. I'm sorry, Ryan. There's nothing we can do about that. Maybe Mr. Hartley will let you visit," she continued, trying to think of anything that might offer some comfort. But her words sounded hollow, and she knew it.

"Maybe," Ryan nodded, leading Prince to the gate. Head bowed, he took the stallion up the path to the back barn. Ty and Amy followed him. Amy felt bad, as though everything was her fault.

"You can't blame yourself, Amy," Ty said softly, as if

he could read her thoughts. "Ryan is much stronger now than when you first met him. You have to remember that. You can change some things, but you can't change everything."

Amy looked up at him and smiled. Maybe Ty was right.

Amy dumped her bag by the door when she came in from school. It was Wednesday, four days after she'd spoken to Luke Norton, and there had been no sign of Mr. Hartley yet.

"Amy! Look at this!" Lou exclaimed as Amy came in. Amy peered over Lou's shoulder.

"It's the new brochure for the Champions bedding," Lou said. "Look at all these photos! They really do a lot to show off Heartland."

Amy took one and studied it briefly. "Looks good," she agreed, handing it back to Lou. She headed for the fridge.

"Is that all you have to say?" Lou asked.

"What else do you want me to say?" Amy couldn't keep the edge of irritation from creeping into her voice. "I said I thought it looked good." She wasn't in the mood to think about brochures — no matter how good they looked. She was feeling so anxious about Prince and Ryan, she could barely think about anything else.

"Thanks a lot," Lou said.

"Sorry, Lou." Amy realized she'd been a little insensitive. "I just keep wishing Mr. Hartley would show up. Then at least we'd know what's going to happen with Prince."

"Well, there's no point in worrying about it," Lou said. "He'll show up when he's ready."

Amy opened her mouth to speak, then shut it again. She and Lou had been getting along really well recently, and she didn't want to spoil it.

"Have you heard from Jess Morgan?" she asked, changing the subject. "She said she was going to let us know about coming to pick up Melody and Daybreak."

"Oh, yes. I was going to tell you," said Lou, brightening. "She's coming tomorrow. I told her you'd want to be here when they go, so she's coming in the late afternoon." Lou smiled.

"OK," said Amy, feeling a little sad. "Thanks, Lou. I guess that means I should do a final session with Daybreak tonight."

❧

Amy changed her usual routine with Daybreak and led her up the path toward the turn-out paddocks for a last tour of the farm. Daybreak, as usual, was curious about everything they passed, and Amy allowed her to investigate an old tractor tire and a pile of straw covered with a tarp. Eventually, she brought the filly to the front yard and began to do T-touch circles along her back, whispering to her as she did so.

"You'll love your new home, Daybreak," she told her. "You've got a great life ahead of you."

Suddenly, Amy became aware of someone watching her, and she looked up. It was Ryan, studying her rhythmic movements as she worked her way up Daybreak's neck.

Amy smiled. "Daybreak's leaving tomorrow," she explained to Ryan. "I'm giving her a final treat."

"Looks like you feel pretty close to her," Ryan said.

Amy looked at him in surprise. She hadn't realized it was so obvious. She nodded, feeling a lump in her throat. "Yeah," she acknowledged. "It's going to be hard to see her go."

"Well," said Ryan. "I guess I'll be going through the same thing myself before long." He smiled bravely. "You've shown me a lot, Amy. If it hadn't been for you, I'd still be stuck in my room. I'm going to make the most of the time I have with Prince, while I still can."

Amy felt moved by his words. Ryan's situation was much, much harder than hers — she still had Heartland, Grandpa, Lou, Ty, and all the other horses. She really admired his courage. "What do you think you'll do when he's gone?" she asked.

Ryan shrugged. "The doctors say I can work again. My left eye's as good as it'll ever be," he said. "So I guess

I'll have to start hunting for something to do. I'd like to find something with horses," he added wistfully. "But that's kind of a long shot."

Amy finished working on Daybreak and led the filly back to her stall. Ryan walked with her. She wished they could offer him work, but Heartland couldn't afford another stable hand. "I'm sure you'll find something, Ryan," she said warmly.

"Yeah, well, we'll see," he said. "Anyway, I'm going to lunge Prince while there's still some daylight."

❧

As Amy settled Daybreak back into her stall, she heard the sound of a car coming up the drive. For a moment she wondered if it was Jess, coming to get Melody and Daybreak a day early. But when the car appeared, she realized she'd never seen it before. She stared at it. She didn't know many people who could afford a Lexus. It must be Mr. Hartley.

Amy hurried forward to greet the man who was getting out of the car. He looked strangely familiar, and Amy suddenly realized where she'd seen him before — on the video of Prince's win last season.

"Mr. Hartley?" she said, extending her hand. "I'm Amy Fleming."

"Nice to meet you, Amy," said the man. "Please call me Dan."

"This is my sister, Lou," Amy added as Lou appeared from the farmhouse. "She's the one who contacted Brookland Ridge." Dan Hartley stepped forward and shook her hand. "It's good to meet you," he said.

"Are you here to see Gallant Prince?" Lou asked.

Dan Hartley nodded. "That's right. How's he doing?"

"Pretty well," Amy said. "I'll take you to see him."

"I'll find Grandpa and Ty," Lou offered.

Amy nodded. She remembered that Ryan had said he was going to lunge Prince. "We'll be down at the training ring," she called over her shoulder, leading the way down the path. Ahead, she could see Prince, trotting around the ring. Despite his characteristic nod, his neck was arched, and his stride looked free and flowing.

"There he is," she said.

Dan Hartley hurried forward, staring at Prince in amazement. "He looks almost like his old self!" he exclaimed as he reached the edge of the ring. Amy wished there had been a way to warn Ryan, but Ryan had already spotted Dan Hartley, and he slowed Prince to a walk, looking anxious.

"Who's that working with him?" asked Dan Hartley, with a puzzled expression. "He looks familiar."

"It's Ryan Bailey," said Amy nervously. "His old stable hand."

"Ryan!" exclaimed Dan Hartley. "So it is. I barely recognized him. The poor guy must have taken the brunt of the flames. I didn't realize — I was just told that he'd left Brookland Ridge for personal reasons."

"He did," Amy admitted. "In a way."

"So what's he doing here?" asked Dan.

"I tracked him down," Amy confessed. "We were having real problems with Prince. He was too locked into his memories of the accident. We realized that only someone who really understood what he'd been through would be able to reach him, so we managed to find Ryan and ask him to come and help us."

She paused as Ryan brought Prince to a perfect square halt in the center of the ring, then she continued in a rush. "Ryan's really speeded up our work. Prince probably would have gotten over his trauma eventually, but we might not have been able to keep him here for that long. Only Ryan could have reached him this fast."

Dan Hartley listened to her words, stroking his chin. "Well," he said, shaking his head. "This is amazing. I never expected to see this kind of change. To be honest, I thought we'd lost Prince for good."

Amy smiled. "We'd like to think that no horse is ever lost for good," she said with feeling. "But there's still a long way to go. We need to make sure that Prince learns to trust other people again. If he'll only work with Ryan, that's no help to you. But we're getting there," she finished as Grandpa, Ty, and Lou joined them.

Dan Hartley looked thoughtful. He leaned on the fence and watched intently as Ryan sent Prince around the ring again on the other rein. He watched them for several minutes. Then, to Amy's surprise, he beckoned to Ryan. Ryan halted Prince again and walked over to the fence, carefully gathering in the longline as he did so.

"Do you remember me, Ryan?" asked Dan Hartley.

"Of course, Mr. Hartley," Ryan said politely. "It's nice to see you."

"You've been doing an amazing job with Prince," said Dan Hartley. "I didn't think he'd make it through. But he has — and Amy tells me it wouldn't have been possible without you."

Ryan looked surprised. "I don't know about that, sir," he said, embarrassed. "Amy persuaded me to come here. I didn't think I could face Prince again. But I'm glad I did. He seems to be nearly his old self again."

Dan Hartley listened to Ryan's words and shook his head. "Well, it's clear to me that you've had a big effect. I don't know how to thank you."

"You don't need to thank me, sir. It's been enough, seeing Prince recover."

"And would it make you happy to see him move on to better things?" Dan Hartley said, studying Ryan's face.

Ryan looked startled. "Well, yes, but —" He trailed off, looking from Mr. Hartley to Amy and back again.

Dan Hartley smiled. "We need you at the stud farm with Prince. Would you consider coming to work there?"

Ryan looked at him, stunned.

"When Prince is ready, that is," Mr. Hartley added. "I know he still needs more time here first. But he'll always need someone to look after him, and you're clearly the best man for the job. I seem to remember you've got a wife who's also pretty good with horses, don't you? I'm sure I could take on two new stable hands if she's interested."

A huge grin spread across Ryan's face. He extended his hand to Dan Hartley. "That's a very generous offer, sir," he said. "I'd be proud to look after Prince for you."

Dan Hartley rubbed his hands together. "Great. I'm glad that's settled," he said, and looked around expectantly at Ty and Grandpa. Quickly, Amy introduced everyone, and they all began walking back up the path toward the farmhouse.

Grandpa walked next to Amy and put his arm around her. "You were right to keep trying, Amy," he said in a low voice. "Things work out for people who believe in themselves — and in others. I think you've shown Ryan that — and the rest of us, too."

Amy stopped and waited for Ryan to bring Prince alongside them. Ryan was still shaking his head in disbelief. "I never expected anything like this could happen," he told them. "I thought everything was over for me."

Amy grinned and reached up to stroke Prince's neck. *No,* she thought. *Everything's just beginning.*

❧

"I'll go and get Melody's blankets," said Ty the next evening, as Jess Morgan stood talking to Lou and Grandpa in the yard. She'd arrived with her horse trailer about an hour after Amy had gotten home from school.

"OK," said Amy. "I'll be in their stall."

She headed for Melody and Daybreak's stall and stood for a moment, looking over the door as Melody pulled hay from her hay net. "Time to go, girls," she said softly.

She let herself in, and Ty appeared with the traveling blankets and boots. They led the pair out and started buckling traveling boots onto Melody's legs. Jess came over and helped them check everything, then took Melody's lead line from Ty.

"Up we go," she said, leading Melody toward the ramp. Melody looked at it fearfully, and Amy remembered that she'd always been nervous about traveling. Amy stepped forward and stroked her neck as Jess talked to her in a calm, soothing voice, reassuring her.

"Good-bye, Melody," Amy whispered. "Go on, girl. You can do it." She smiled at Jess when, after a few nervous snorts, Melody followed her up the ramp.

Then it was Daybreak's turn. Amy knelt quickly at the filly's side and hugged her. Daybreak nudged Amy with her muzzle.

"Good-bye, Daybreak," Amy whispered, tears blurring her eyes. With a final kiss on the filly's soft nose, Amy blinked back her tears and stood up, handing Jess her lead line. She knew there would be more Melodys and more Daybreaks — mares needing help through their pain, foals needing guidance and encouragement — but none of them would touch her heart quite like this little filly. As she stepped back, Amy knew she was saying good-bye to another part of her family.

Jess showed Daybreak the ramp, and Daybreak sniffed at it curiously. Then she stepped onto it willingly, eager to join her mother. Amy took one last look inside the trailer. Daybreak turned and regarded her with bright, inquisitive eyes. With a gentle whinny, the filly seemed to say good-bye as Jess slowly lifted the ramp.

Grandpa came and held Amy's hand as Ty helped Jess slot the final bolts into place. Lou stepped forward, and Grandpa put his other hand on her shoulder.

"Thank you for giving me two wonderful horses," Jess said.

Amy smiled as Jess climbed up into the driver's seat.

"That's what we're here for," she said. "Thanks for promising to take care of them. I promise I'll come to visit Daybreak soon."

Jess nodded as she started the engine. Amy waved and smiled, her heart filling with happiness as she realized that Daybreak would still be out there, and that in her place at Heartland, there would soon be another horse — a horse that needed her and whose life would be changed for the better.

Heartland™

Healing horses, healing hearts...

Unbridle the Power of Heartland...

❏ BFF	0-439-13020-4	**#1: Coming Home**	$4.50 US
❏ BFF	0-439-13022-0	**#2: After the Storm**	$4.50 US
❏ BFF	0-439-13024-7	**#3: Breaking Free**	$4.50 US
❏ BFF	0-439-13025-5	**#4: Taking Chances**	$4.50 US
❏ BFF	0-439-13026-3	**#5: Come What May**	$4.50 US
❏ BFF	0-439-13035-2	**#6: One Day You'll Know**	$4.50 US
❏ BFF	0-439-31714-2	**#7: Out of the Darkness**	$4.50 US

Available wherever you buy books, or use this order form.

Scholastic Inc., P.O. Box 7502, Jefferson City, MO 65102

Please send me the books I have checked above. I am enclosing $_____ (please add $2.00 to cover shipping and handling). Send check or money order—no cash or C.O.D.s please.

Name_____ Birth date_____

Address_____

City_____ State/Zip_____

Please allow four to six weeks for delivery. Offer good in U.S.A. only. Sorry, mail orders are not available to residents of Canada. Prices subject to change.

www.scholastic.com

■ SCHOLASTIC

HR202